The Nameless Hero

Also by Lee Bacon

JOSHUA DREAD

JOSHUA DREAD

The Nameless Hero

LEE BACON

DELACORTE PRESS

Text copyright © 2013 by Lee Bacon
Jacket art and interior illustrations copyright © 2013 by Brandon Dorman

All rights reserved. Published in the United States by Delacorte Press, an imprint of Random House Children's Books, a division of Random House, Inc., New York.

Delacorte Press is a registered trademark and the colophon is a trademark of Random House, Inc.

Visit us on the Web! randomhouse.com/kids

Educators and librarians, for a variety of teaching tools, visit us at RHTeachersLibrarians.com

Library of Congress Cataloging-in-Publication Data
Bacon, Lee.
The nameless hero / Lee Bacon. — First edition.
pages cm — (Joshua Dread)
Summary: Joshua Dread accepts an invitation from Gyfted & Talented, a summer program for children with superpowers, but he and his friends have been chosen to form the greatest superhero team of all time, and their newfound fame could mean big trouble with Joshua's supervillain parents.
ISBN 978-0-385-74186-6 (hardback) — ISBN 978-0-375-99028-1 (glb) — ISBN 978-0-375-98722-9 (ebook) [1. Supervillains—Fiction. 2. Superheroes—Fiction. 3. Camps—Fiction. 4. Friendship—Fiction. 5. Fame—Fiction.] I. Title.
PZ7.B13446Nam 2013
[Fic]—dc23
2013003310

The text of this book is set in 12-point Cochin.

Book design by Trish Parcell

Printed in the United States of America

10 9 8 7 6 5 4 3 2 1

First Edition

Random House Children's Books
supports the First Amendment and celebrates the right to read.

For my parents

The Nameless Hero

1

The last day of the sixth grade wasn't turning out the way I'd expected at all. And that was *before* the substitute librarian tried to kill me.

I was in my room, looking for something to wear, when an explosion rocked the floor beneath me. Whatever it was, I had a feeling my mom and dad were involved.

Take it from me, when you have supervillains for parents, you get used to unexplained noises in the house. It might've been a new invention my dad was testing out. Or maybe one of my mom's experiments had gone terribly wrong.

Either way, I wasn't going to let it bother me. Not on a day like this. The school year was finally coming to an end. Summer was right around the corner.

Just the thought of it made me smile. Two and a half months of sleeping late and watching TV, not worrying about homework or schedules. Two and a half months of nothing.

If only I'd known how wrong I was.

My dad was seated at the dining room table, drinking coffee and reading the newspaper. Strands of morning sunlight shone through the window, reflecting off the abnormally thick rims of the glasses he'd customized to regulate his super-vision.

"Morning, Joshua," he said.

"Hey, did you hear a noise a minute ago?"

"Noise? What kind of noise?"

Before I could answer, another crash erupted. It sounded like it had come from the kitchen.

"*That* kind of noise," I said. "What was that?"

"Oh, that's just Elliot," Dad said. "He's making pancakes."

All of a sudden, a robot lurched into the room. He looked a little like a tin trash can, with protractible arms on either side of his body and flat paddles for feet. His head was a cube-shaped hunk of metal that wobbled on top of a thin plastic neck.

Elliot had made his entrance.

Dad had come up with the idea for Elliot after sharing a ride with Captain Justice seven months earlier. It had been awkward enough for my parents to carpool with their sworn enemy, the superhero they'd been fighting for years. On top of that, Dad had also seemed a little jealous of Stanley, Captain Justice's robot butler in the driver's seat.

"Why can't *we* have a robot butler?" Dad had complained once we'd gotten home. "We're two of the most successful supervillains in the world, right?"

"Of course, honey," Mom had said, massaging the back of his neck.

"Then we deserve a robot butler too!"

And so Dad had set out to build one. But the thing about my dad is, when he gets really excited about an idea, he becomes kind of impatient. It's part of the reason why our house is so packed with inventions. He's always working on five things at once. And it's also part of the reason why all these inventions are usually a little bit . . . flawed.

Elliot was a good example. He'd only been in service for a couple of weeks, but he'd already destroyed half our house. He'd smashed the front window during his attempt to clean it. The living room rug had been torn to shreds as a result of his "vacuuming."

Breakfast didn't seem like it was going to turn out any better.

"The pancakes look delicious," Dad said to Elliot.

I glanced at the charred brown mush that Elliot was carrying. It looked more like grilled boogers than pancakes. But Dad just went on talking to Elliot like he was the best robot butler in the world.

3

"Thank you for preparing breakfast," he said.

"You are welcooooome," said Elliot in a slurred electronic voice. "It was my pleasummmmack!"

Did I mention that whenever Elliot spoke, his voice came out sounding like a radio going haywire? Dad kept promising to fix the robot's speech function. Obviously, he hadn't gotten around to it yet.

Elliot set down one of the plates on the edge of the table. The other plate missed the table and crashed to the ground in an explosion of porcelain shards and lumpy batter. He looked up at my dad with his big glowing eyes.

"My apologies, Mr. Dormmmilack."

"That's quite all right, Elliot. And my name is pronounced *Dominick. Do-mi-nick.*"

"Yes, sir, Mr. Dummy-neck."

"Close enough," Dad said in a reassuring tone.

We both watched as Elliot attempted to pick up the shards of broken plate, tearing out several large chunks of the dining room floor in the process.

"It's important to remain encouraging," Dad whispered to me as Elliot tottered back into the kitchen, scattering pieces of porcelain behind him. "I really do think he's made some progress."

A crash rang out from the kitchen. It sounded like an entire drawer of silverware had been dumped on the floor.

"I'd better go check on that," Dad said, jogging through the door.

A moment after Dad left the dining room, Mom entered. "Morning!"

ELLIOT

Having a robot butler isn't nearly as cool as it sounds. Most of the time, Elliot's attempts to tidy up around the house result in widespread destruction.

She leaned against the doorframe, her long black hair still wet from the shower. Her green eyes crinkled at the sides as she smiled at me.

"What happened here?" she asked, glancing down at the smashed plate and the missing sections of the floor.

"Elliot," I said.

Mom nodded. No need for further explanation.

"He's in the kitchen with Dad right now." I could hear the muffled sound of Dad speaking encouragingly to Elliot. "How long are we gonna have to put up with that thing?" I asked.

"Which thing?" Mom asked. "The robot or your dad?"

"I was referring to the robot."

She let out an exhausted sigh.

"This is important to your father," she said. "So I think we have to support him."

"But why do we even need a robot butler in the first place?"

"Ever since that ride with Captain Justice, your father has—" Mom glanced toward the kitchen and lowered her voice. "He's felt a little . . . *insecure*."

I heard the rumble of drawers opening and closing. My dad's voice called out, "No, Elliot. Please don't put the cheese grater in your mouth!"

Mom took a deep breath and exhaled slowly. "This hasn't been easy for either of us, you know. We spent the last ten years fighting with Captain Justice. Now we're not sure how we're supposed to feel about him."

I couldn't deny that my parents had been acting unusual

6

for the past seven months. At least by their standards. Neither of them had been involved in a single attempt to destroy the world. Not even a *continent*.

It was bizarre.

Don't get me wrong. I was happy to see my parents considering other career options. For as long as I could remember, I'd known that they were different from other parents. And not different in a good way. More like they were different in a molten-lava-is-about-to-wipe-out-New-Jersey-and-it's-all-their-fault kind of way.

All along, I hoped they would find jobs that were more normal. Or at least less evil.

Now it looked like that was exactly what they'd done. Over the past seven months, Mom hadn't once used her power to control vegetation as a part of any supervillainous schemes. Instead, she'd been totally caught up in her job as a horticulture professor at Sheepsdale Community College.

And as for Dad—well, lately he'd been devoting all his time to Elliot.

"No, Elliot!" Dad called out from the kitchen. "Put the refrigerator down!"

This was followed by a *clump* and a howl of pain from my dad.

"YAARGH!" he screamed. "Not on my TOE!"

"Soooorry, Mr. Dummy-neck."

Mom rolled her eyes. "Just try to be patient. And let your dad know I'll be skipping breakfast this morning. Have to get to campus early to grade finals."

As soon as Mom swept out of the dining room, Dad hobbled into it. "I've got to find a bandage for my toe," he said. "Looks like you'll have to eat without me."

As he limped out the door, I glanced down at the burned mush waiting for me on my plate.

"Yum," I muttered.

When I got to the bus stop, I unzipped my backpack and pulled out the Sheepsdale Middle School yearbook. I'd received it the day before, just like everyone else in school.

I opened the book and flipped through until I found my picture. I was the skinny kid in the lower right-hand part of the page who looked like he'd just been stumped by a tough math question. My disheveled brown hair blended perfectly with a shadow in the background, making it look like I had a huge lopsided Afro.

Otherwise, it was a great picture.

There was a name printed beneath the photo, but it wasn't my name. At least, not my real name. Part of being the child of two notorious supervillains is hiding your identity. People still called me Joshua, but only a few people—my parents, Milton, Sophie—knew that my actual last name was Dread.

It can be tough to live with a false identity, to switch your names the way other people switch shoes. But just like everything else in life, after a while, you get used to it. Soon you mostly forget that you were ever anyone else.

I closed the yearbook with a sharp crack and shoved it inside my backpack. As I did, a slip of paper fell out. It fluttered for a second in the air, then landed next to my foot. I bent down to pick it up.

The paper was small, about the size of a postcard. One side was blank. I was about to toss it into the trash can, when I noticed what was printed on the other side:

YOU ARE THE CHOSEN.

I stared at the words, my mind spinning to make sense of them. *The chosen?* What was that supposed to mean?

I nearly dropped the slip of paper when I heard a voice behind me.

"Hey, Joshua."

I spun around and saw Milton. Tall and thin, with sandy blond hair that never seemed to stay in place, Milton had been my closest friend ever since I'd moved in down the street from him nearly three years earlier. Even after learning that my parents were the Dread Duo, he still treated me the same as he did before. Well, pretty much the same. Every once in a while, he asked to borrow my dad's plasma gun.

"I've got big plans for our first week of summer," Milton said. "On Monday, we can go to AwesomeWorld. That new amusement park outside town? They have a ride there that's so extreme, if you don't puke, you get your money back!"

"That sounds . . . great," I said, hardly listening. My

thoughts were still coiled around the slip of paper in my hand. *You are the chosen.* How could it have gotten into my backpack without my knowing about it? And what did it mean?

Chosen for *what*?

As the bus pulled up, I gripped the note a little more tightly in my fist. All of a sudden, I had a feeling that my plans for a relaxing, stress-free summer had just gone up in flames.

2

On my way to school, I made up my mind. The note must've been a prank. And I had an idea who was behind it.

Joey Birch and Brick Gristol.

The two of them had been picking on me since my first day at Sheepsdale Middle School. They'd probably snuck the note into my backpack the day before when I wasn't looking. No telling what it was supposed to mean, but if Joey and Brick were involved, I was sure they had something unpleasant in mind.

A few minutes before first period, I caught up with them in the hallway. Joey had red hair and a permanent scowl on his face. It was easy to spot Brick standing next to him, since he was about a head taller than anyone else in our grade. Brick was shaped like a refrigerator (except uglier), with a mouthful of crooked teeth and a buzz cut. At the moment, he was holding a fifth grader upside down by the ankles.

I stepped toward them. Joey, Brick, and the upside-down fifth grader all looked my way. "I know about the note," I said.

"Listen, Dorkface," Joey said. "I have no idea what you're talking about. Besides, me and Brick are kind of in the middle of something right now."

He nodded at the upside-down fifth grader in Brick's grip. The fifth grader waved at me.

For a split second, I wondered if he was telling the truth. But if it wasn't them, then how had the note ended up in my backpack? It's not like it could have just *appeared* there.

"There's no point lying," I said. "I know it was you."

Joey turned to where Brick was standing. "You know anything about a note?"

Brick and the fifth grader both shook their heads.

Joey looked back to me. "See? We don't know what you're talking about. Now why don't you get out of here before we *make* you?"

Joey's sneer deepened. He took a step in my direction.

A feeling came over me—at once familiar and completely strange. See, my parents aren't the only ones in the family who have superpowers. Earlier in the school year, I'd learned that I was Gyfted, which is another way of saying that freaky things sometimes happen to me. And I'm not just talking about puberty. I have the power of spontaneous combustion. Basically, it means that I can make things blow up. Spontaneously.

12

My Gyft kicks in whenever I concentrate really hard or get too stressed out about something. My fingertips start to tingle, and a rush of adrenaline shoots through my body. Blood surges through my veins, and my heart pounds so hard that it feels like it might burst out of my chest any second. These are the warning signs that something's about to spontaneously combust.

And I was feeling all of them right then.

But before I had a chance to test out my power on Joey and Brick, another voice cut into the group.

"Hi, guys."

Sophie was standing beside us. I guess you could say Sophie was one of my best friends from school. She was also Captain Justice's daughter. As soon as Joey saw her, worry flashed across his features. Brick took a step back, trembling so much that the fifth grader in his hands began to shake.

Sophie was a slight, wispy girl with blue-gray eyes and blond hair that hung to her shoulders. You might think it's a little odd that a girl like this could cause such a reaction from the school's two biggest bullies. But Sophie was also born with a Gyft. And if you'd ever seen her power in action, you'd know she can cause some serious damage. Earlier in the school year, Joey and Brick had experienced this firsthand. Ever since, they'd done their best to avoid her.

Sophie took a step forward, and Brick released his grip on the fifth grader. The kid fell to the ground, then scrambled away.

"C'mon, Brick." Joey's voice cracked. "We don't have

SOPHIE

Sophie may look small,
but she packs a BIG punch.

time to mess around with a couple of—of freaks." His eyes swept over both of us. His expression was a mixture of disgust and fear.

Brick was already backing away. Joey followed him. Without another word, they turned and vanished into the crowd.

"What was that all about?" Sophie asked once they were out of sight.

"I was asking them about this prank they tried to pull on me." I told her about what I'd found in my backpack. As soon as I mentioned the note, Sophie's expression changed.

"You found one too?" She reached into her pocket and pulled out a slip of paper. It was exactly the same size as the one I'd found a little while before. And the words printed on it were also the same.

YOU ARE THE CHOSEN.

I could've believed that Joey and Brick would sneak it into my backpack. But they were way too intimidated by Sophie to try to play a trick on her. It couldn't be them. So then, if they didn't do it . . . who did?

The final class for the day—and the entire school year—was American history with Ms. McGirt. Instead of meeting in her classroom as usual, we'd all gathered in the library for her lesson on library orientation.

I guess Ms. McGirt was unaware that the last class on

the last day of school was the absolute *worst* time to teach us about navigating the library. Most kids were more interested in watching the clock above her shoulder, the seconds ticking away toward summer. Not that Ms. McGirt noticed. Truth is, she didn't notice much of anything.

She was standing in front of a tall shelf of books, blinking dazedly in our general direction. Her eyes were magnified behind a thick pair of glasses. Her white hair was pulled into a tight bun.

A student in front of me called out a question, but Ms. McGirt ignored it—probably because she didn't hear it. (She was mostly deaf.) Instead, she turned to her right and began lecturing a stack of encyclopedias on how to use the online catalog system. (She was pretty blind too.)

I was seated at a table with Sophie and Milton. Joey and Brick were a few tables away. Behind them was the desk where the librarian usually stood. But she must've been out for the day, because another woman was standing in her place.

The substitute librarian was a sickly-looking woman with a horribly hunched back and grim features. Dark bags hung under her eyes. Her skin was gray. The only part of her face that seemed to have any color was her mouth. Her lips were smeared with bright red lipstick.

She was slouched behind the long desk, scanning books, one after the other. The machine let out a *beep* every time a new book was scanned. I gasped as a clump of gray hair fell loose from her head and landed on top of a pile of books in front of her. Without seeming to notice, she grabbed the tangle of hair and swiped it across the scanner.

Beep.

She went on scanning like nothing had happened. And as if that weren't gross enough already, when she looked up from her work, her dark eyes landed on me. She licked her red lips with an expression in her eyes that looked almost . . .

Hungry.

I glanced down at my desk, trying to shake off the disturbing thought. My mind must've been playing tricks on me. That was all. Just a bad case of ESF (Extreme School Fatigue). And the cure would come at the end of this class. Summer was just around the corner. I just had to make it till then.

And yet every time I caught sight of the substitute librarian, a chill ran down my spine. I tried to concentrate on Ms. McGirt's lesson. But it's hard enough to pay attention to Ms. McGirt on a normal day. It was basically impossible with a creepy substitute librarian staring me down like she wanted to make me her afternoon snack.

"For the rest of the class, you are free to explore the library," Ms. McGirt said to the encyclopedias in front of her.

The class got up from their tables and began moving through the stacks. Joey shot me a dirty look, but it seemed tame compared to the way the librarian was still glaring at me.

I stood from the table and quickly made my way between two tall rows of books. Sophie and Milton followed.

"Hey, wait up!" Milton called, power walking to catch up with me. "What's the big hurry?"

I stopped when we reached an isolated corner of the library. Now that the librarian was out of sight, I realized how foolish I was acting. Was I actually running away from an old lady? In a library?

"Okay, so I guess we're supposed to look through a few books," Sophie said, glancing at the shelf beside us.

"I can't believe Ms. McGirt wanted to have class *here*," Milton said, grabbing a book at random. "There should be a law against teaching anything on the last day of school."

Above the sound of their conversation, I could hear a noise from somewhere else in the library. A quiet, steady squeak.

"Do you hear that?" I asked.

"Hear *what*?"

I listened for the noise, but now it seemed to be gone. There was only the slight, distant murmur of voices and the low rumble of the air conditioner.

"Um—never mind," I said. "Guess I'm just hearing things."

I glanced at the table in front of me. There in the middle of the table was a book. It was odd. An instant earlier, I could've sworn there was nothing on the table. So now I was hearing things *and* seeing things.

At least school was nearly over. I obviously needed the break.

I picked up the book. When I opened it, something fell loose and landed on the table.

A slip of paper.

I took the slip between my fingers and stared down at the words printed across one side:

PREPARE YOURSELF. YOU ARE IN DANGER.

Pulling my eyes away from the words, I glanced up. Sophie was standing beside me, a very odd look on her face. She was holding a little white slip of paper too. And from where I was standing, I could just make out the exact same text printed on one side.

I had about a million questions pounding in my temples. Where did these notes keep coming from? Why was it that only Sophie and I were finding them?

Over the sound of these questions, I heard the noise again. The steady squeak. This time I was sure it wasn't just in my head. Judging by the looks on Sophie's and Milton's faces, they heard it this time too.

The noise grew louder. *Squeeeaaak.*

It was getting closer.

A form appeared at the end of a row of books. The substitute librarian. She was pushing a cart of books with a loose wheel. When she spotted us, she brought the cart to a halt, and the squeaking stopped. Her head swiveled and she glared in our direction.

Her skin was a pale gray, the color of concrete. The hump on her back looked even worse than it had before, bulging from beneath her blouse. Where her eyes should've been, there were dark pools of shadows sunken into her face. And I didn't think that was red lipstick smeared around her mouth after all. It looked more like blood.

The librarian opened her mouth, and that was when I noticed her teeth. They were as sharp as daggers.

"Did you forget about an overdue book or something?" Milton asked me in a shaky voice. "'Cause the librarian looks seriously ticked off."

"That's not a librarian," Sophie whispered. "She looks like a Cross-Species Hybrid Mutation. Part shark, part human. I saw something similar attack my dad a few months back. Just stay perfectly still. Mutants are drawn to sudden movements."

"Perfectly still," Milton repeated. "Got it."

My heart pounded. A bead of sweat dripped down my cheek. But I followed Sophie's advice, remaining frozen in place. And the thing is . . . it actually seemed to work. The mutant's eyes began to wander, as if she'd lost track of us. She took a step to the side, glancing over her shoulder.

And then the bell rang. We must've been so wound up with tension that the sudden noise was like an eject button in our brains. The three of us jumped about ten feet into the air.

The mutant's eyes snapped back to us. An instant later, she was roaring in our direction.

3

Of all the days to get mauled by a mutant librarian, why did it have to be the last day of school?

Kids were flooding the hallways and celebrating their new freedom, but Sophie, Milton, and I had something else to think about. The librarian surged toward us, gnashing her pointed teeth. She lifted the book cart off the ground and heaved it at Sophie.

Before I even realized what I was doing, I dove toward Sophie and collided with her a split second before the airborne book cart would have hit her. We both collapsed to the ground just as the cart crashed against the wall behind us.

The librarian howled in anger. Or maybe she was just hungry. It's tough to tell with mutants.

The cart was lying in a pile of spilled books behind me. I grabbed it and hurled it with all my strength at the librarian. At the same moment, I felt a jolt of energy blasting in my veins. Spontaneous combustion coursed through my entire body, turning the cart into a blazing tornado of metal and books.

The cart exploded, and the librarian collapsed to the ground, moaning.

Out of the corner of my eye, I could tell that Sophie's Gyft had just kicked in. Her power of superstrength came with a side effect that was tough to miss. Her skin was glowing brightly, making her look like a human lightbulb.

"Look out!" she screamed.

The librarian was already on her feet again. Part of her blouse had been burned away, revealing a silvery shark's fin jutting from her spine. So that was why she'd looked so hunched. It wasn't bad posture. Her shark side was poking through.

"RRAAAAARGHHH!" the mutant roared, lunging toward me. I would've ended up shark meat if it weren't for Sophie. She grabbed hold of a bookshelf that was nearly twice her height and heaved it over her shoulder like it weighed nothing.

"Joshua!" she screamed. "DUCK!"

I dropped to my knees. Books flew everywhere as Sophie swung the shelf like a baseball bat. A whoosh of air swept over my head, and then a loud *craaack* reverberated in my ears. The shelf connected with the librarian, sending her spinning through the air. She collided with a wall and landed on the ground in a heap of books.

Ordinarily this kind of commotion would've sent dozens

of kids and teachers running to investigate what had just happened. But right then the rest of the school was too occupied with the start of summer.

Sophie helped me to my feet. Her skin was glowing so brightly that it burned my eyes to look directly at her.

"Any idea why a mutant librarian is trying to kill us?" Milton asked.

"No clue," I said. "Whatever's going on, those notes must've been from someone who knew this was gonna happen."

"But that's impossible," Sophie said. "How could a note inside a book—"

She stopped speaking when a fierce growl ripped through the room. The librarian was glaring at us with her dark eyes. She rose from the pile of charred books and debris, baring her razor-sharp teeth. All the damage we'd inflicted had only made her angrier.

I wasn't sure how much longer we could hold out. We needed another strategy. I caught sight of the row of windows lining the wall.

"I might have an idea," I said to Sophie and Milton. "Just stay here."

"Why? What're you—"

Before they could say any more, I set off toward the window. On the way, I grabbed a red book off the shelf and flapped it above my head.

"Here, sharkey-sharkey!" I called.

The librarian stopped stalking toward Sophie and Milton. Now she was staring at me.

THE MUTANT LIBRARIAN

This substitute librarian is capable
of inflicting some serious pain—
and not just with late fees.

"GROOGGG?" she said.

"Ooh, real scary." I took my place in front of the windows. "Is that the best you've got?"

The monstrous woman responded with a noise—half scream, half roar—that vibrated in my bones. Note to self: never taunt a mutant.

She set off toward me, her silver fin cutting through the air like a knife. Every muscle of my body wanted to get out of there, but I stood my ground, baiting her with the book.

In my mind, I repeated Sophie's advice from earlier. *Mutants are drawn to sudden movements.* I wasn't exactly thrilled to be testing out her hypothesis with my life, but at least it seemed to be working. The flapping red encyclopedia in my hands was driving the librarian wild. She ripped across the room, a gray blur of gnashing teeth that got closer and closer with each heartbeat.

"Run, Joshua!" Milton screamed. "Get out of there!"

Not yet, I told myself. *Not quite yet.*

The mutant's jaws opened wide. She launched into the air.

I dove sideways and hit the ground just as the librarian went sailing through the window. There was the sound of glass shattering. Then she was gone.

"Well, that was a nice way to spend our last day of school," Milton said.

The three of us were gathered at the broken window, looking down at the parking lot below. The librarian was gone. Although Principal Sloane probably wasn't going to be happy when he saw the mutant-shaped dent in the hood of his car.

"What's that?" Milton pointed at the windowsill. Two cream-white envelopes were lying there side by side. One had my name written on it. The other had Sophie's.

I was positive they hadn't been there a moment earlier.

I grabbed hold of the envelope with my name, and Sophie took hers. Pressing my finger beneath the seal, I tore it open.

Inside was a slip of paper. It was exactly the same size as those I'd found earlier in the day, but this one had more written on it. My hands still trembling from everything we'd just been through, I stared down at the words.

~~~~~~

CONGRATULATIONS!
YOU ARE INVITED TO ATTEND
GYFTED & TALENTED
THE BUS WILL ARRIVE AT THE FOLLOWING LOCATION AND TIME:
WHERE: YOUR HOUSE
WHEN: IN ONE WEEK
PS: BE READY EARLY
(PPS: VERY EARLY)
PLEASE PRESENT THIS INVITATION TO GAIN ENTRANCE.

~~~~~~

4

"**G**yfted and Talented? What the heck is *that*?"

Sophie and Milton looked back at me blankly. It was just one more question to toss on top of all the other questions that had been piling up that day. Like . . . how did those notes keep appearing out of nowhere? And was there any particular reason why the substitute librarian had just tried to kill us?

"Hey," Milton asked, "can I borrow one of those notes for a second?"

"Sure." I distractedly handed him my slip of paper.

He turned and wandered between a row of books, out of sight.

"This is really weird." Sophie was staring at her own slip. "What should we do?"

My instinct was to throw the note away and do my best

to forget all about it. But I could already see the spark of interest flaring in Sophie's eyes.

"You aren't actually thinking about *doing* this, are you?" I asked.

"Aren't you at least *curious*? This invitation must be pretty important, after all the trouble they went through getting it to us."

"All the trouble? Are you referring to the invasion of privacy or the mutant shark lady that just attacked us?"

"Look, it says here we've got a week to decide. I just think we should keep an open mind."

"Fine. I'll think about it."

"Great!" Sophie smiled. "So where did Milton go? He was just—"

"Hey, guys." Milton popped out from behind a shelf of books with an odd expression on his face.

"There you are," Sophie said. "What were you doing?"

"Nothing." The odd expression grew odder. "Just—you know—securing the area. Making sure there aren't any other monsters roaming around."

"But why did you take the—"

"We should probably get out of here." Milton handed the note back to me. "I mean—before anyone comes around asking why the library is such a wreck."

Milton was definitely acting strange, but he had a point. Our corner of the library looked like a disaster zone.

"Well, we missed our bus." I turned to Sophie. "Mind if we catch a ride with you?"

Sophie punched a button on her phone. "Stanley's on his way."

When Stanley arrived five minutes later, I could hardly believe my eyes. He pulled up in a shining black limo.

"The SUV's in the shop having a flamethrower replaced," Sophie explained, like that was the most normal thing in the world.

Milton and I climbed in through the back door, gaping. A long row of leather seats stretched along one side. On the other side was a mini-fridge, a flat-screen TV, and a built-in computer.

Stanley was in the driver's seat. He glanced back at us, the sunlight reflecting off his smooth, metallic skin. He was wearing a bow tie and a chauffeur's hat.

"Greetings, children," he said in a smooth, automated voice.

Stanley had been the inspiration for Elliot. But except for the fact that they were both robots, the two of them had nothing in common. Stanley was tall and slender, while Elliot was squat and stumpy. Elliot had none of the cool features that Stanley had (unless you consider the ability to eat every fork in the silverware drawer cool).

Stanley turned in his seat, looking back at Sophie. "Your father notified me that he will be late this evening."

A disappointed look came over Sophie's face. "Again?"

"Yes, Miss Justice. The filming is apparently taking longer than expected."

Milton jumped forward on his seat like he'd just been shocked. "Filming! What kind of filming?" His voice was loud with excitement. "Is Captain Justice, like, shooting a movie or something?"

Milton got this way whenever Captain Justice was mentioned. He couldn't really help it. He was a huge fan.

"He's not shooting a movie," Sophie said. "It's a different kind of project."

"What *kind* of project?" Milton persisted.

Sophie's hands bunched in her lap. An embarrassed expression crossed her face. "It's nothing, really. Just a"—she lowered her voice—"a reality show."

Milton jumped so high that he bumped his head against the sunroof. "Awesome! I can't wait to see it! When are they gonna show it on TV? Can I be in it?"

Sophie obviously didn't share Milton's enthusiasm. She only stared out the tinted window at the scenery passing by. When she did finally speak, her voice was quiet and distant.

"My dad wasn't home much *before* this show," she said. "Now he has to get up extra early to meet with wardrobe and makeup people. Before, he was at least around the house *sometimes*—you know, when there weren't any major crimes or photo shoots. But now . . ."

Sophie took a breath, her eyes peering out the window.

"I guess I never really expected a normal life. Not with my dad being . . . well—*my dad*. But sometimes, I feel like he doesn't even know I'm there."

I tried to think of something that would make Sophie feel better. At least her dad was a superhero. Try being the child of supervillains. Every time *my* parents got caught up in a plan, I had to worry that the world was going to end up annihilated.

Not to mention that Sophie had a way more qualified robot butler. That had to count for something, right? And he even knew just the right thing to say that would lift everyone's spirits.

"Perhaps you children would like to see what's in the mini-fridge," Stanley suggested.

"Ooh, can we?" Milton asked excitedly.

This brought a slight smile to Sophie's lips. She opened the door to the sleek silver mini-fridge. It was stocked with soda, orange juice, and sparkling water.

After that, everyone's mood improved. We explored the rest of the limo, discovering that every seat came with a built-in control panel.

"What does this button do?" I asked, pointing at the panel next to my seat.

"That turns up the air-conditioning," Sophie said.

"And this?"

"That one makes your seat eject two hundred feet into the air."

I held my control panel a little more carefully after that.

Sophie explained a few of the other buttons. She leaned toward me, close enough that her hair brushed against my shoulder.

"This one makes hundreds of robot bees shoot out of the

exhaust pipe," she said, pointing. "And this enables the energy shield. Oh, and here's a cool one—"

Sophie reached forward and pressed one of the buttons on my control panel. I gripped my armrest a little more tightly, halfway expecting my seat to eject into the air or burst into flames. Instead, a shining disco ball lowered from the vehicle's ceiling and shades unfolded to cover the windows. Once it was dark inside the limo, lights began blinking rapidly.

"It's a strobe light!" Sophie said.

I waved my hand in front of my face. The blinking light made the motions look jerky and disjointed.

"Look at me!" Milton said. He was doing the robot.

Sophie and I couldn't stop laughing. Even Stanley seemed impressed, which was especially nice, considering he was an actual robot.

Sophie hit a couple of other buttons on the control panel. Music blared through the limo, and the sunroof slid open. The three of us stood up with our heads sticking out the open roof, the wind rushing through our hair.

We were having such a good time that I hardly noticed when we pulled up to the street that Milton and I lived on.

"I've got to show you something," Milton said once the limo had driven away. He shoved his hand into his pocket

and pulled out a slip of paper that looked exactly like the
ones Sophie and I had received. I skimmed the words at
the top of the note.

CONGRATULATIONS!
YOU ARE INVITED TO ATTEND
GYFTED & TALENTED

"Hold on." I gave the note a closer inspection. "How'd
you—"

And then it occurred to me. Back in the library, when
Milton had asked to borrow one of the notes, Sophie had
wondered where he'd disappeared to. Now I knew—he'd
gone to use the copy machine. He'd created a note for himself.

"Do you think that'll work?" I asked. "Whoever sent
these notes probably knows who received one and who
didn't. They probably have, like, a list or—"

"I had to do *something*," Milton said, his voice cracking.
"You and Sophie—you get to have cool superpowers. You
find mysterious notes. None of that happens for me. I just
don't . . ." Milton paused, glancing away. "I just don't want
to be left out."

It's weird how you can get so tangled up in your own
head that you forget to think about anyone else. All the
time I spent worrying about why I was receiving these
notes, Milton was worrying about why he *wasn't*.

Back at home, my parents were waiting for me in the dining room. And so was Micus. I'd been trying (unsuccessfully) to convince them to move Micus somewhere else, preferably someplace where I'd never see him again.

Micus was the mutant houseplant my mom had created. He also hated my guts. Whenever I got near, he would slap me with his leafy arms or throw clumps of dirt at my head. And any time I tried to retaliate, Mom got mad at *me*, not Micus.

Entering the dining room, I twisted sideways to avoid being grabbed by one of Micus's branches. That was when I saw my parents seated at the table. Between them was a white envelope. By the looks of it, there was a family meeting in session, and I was the last to arrive.

"Hi, Joshua," Mom said. "How was the last day of school?"

I thought for a second about how to answer that. I'd decided not to tell my parents about the whole almost-getting-mauled-by-a-mutant-librarian thing. They had a tendency to pick up and move to a new town whenever there was even a *hint* that trouble was coming.

You could say it was part of the supervillain lifestyle. I'd spent most of my life in constant shuffle. One day, everything was fine. And the next . . . pack your bags. New town, new school, new identity.

But the last three years had been different. We'd stayed in Sheepsdale long enough for me to get settled into a normal life. Or as normal as life can get when the houseplant tries to give you a wedgie every time you get close enough.

I actually had friends. And one little attack could change all that. So I'd decided not to mention it. At least, not yet.

"School was fine." I shrugged, dropping my backpack to the floor. "I survived, anyway."

"Excellent!"

My eyes landed on the envelope that was lying on the table. "What's that?"

"See for yourself." Dad slid the envelope across the table.

Everyone was receiving letters today. The envelope was addressed to my parents, although I noticed that there was no stamp and no return address. Inside were a one-page letter and a glossy brochure. I picked up the letter and started to read:

Dear Parent(s) and/or Guardian(s),

Congratulations! Your child has been selected to attend Gyfted & Talented, an exclusive two-month summer program specifically intended for boys and girls with extraordinary Gyfts.

I stared at the page, bewildered. So that was what this was all about? A summer camp for Gyfted kids?

I opened the brochure, and my eyes scanned colorful photographs of kids practicing their Gyfts, riding around a track on hover skateboards, hanging out around a holographic campfire.

On the last page of the brochure, oversized letters stretched across the glossy page:

GYFTED & TALENTED

MASTER YOUR GYFTS, TRAIN WITH EXPERTS,
GET FIRSTHAND EXPERIENCE.
AND WHILE YOU'RE AT IT,
MAYBE YOU'LL EVEN SAVE THE WORLD!

"'Save the world'?" I said, reading the last line out loud. That didn't sound like the kind of thing my parents would be into, considering they'd devoted their careers to doing the exact opposite. But surprisingly, they didn't seem to mind.

"I'm sure it's just a figure of speech," Mom said breezily.

"Probably their way of being politically correct," Dad added. "It's not like they could come out in favor of *ending* the world."

"But it sounds like it might be intended for . . . you know . . . superheroes," I pointed out.

"Let's not focus on labeling everything," Mom said. "Hero, villain—at your age, the most important thing is to figure out how to best use your Gyft. You still have plenty of time to realize what a great supervillain you'll be."

"So you want me to go?"

Mom and Dad exchanged a glance that let me know they'd already talked it over. After clearing his throat, Dad said, "Your mother and I feel that it would be a good opportunity. A chance to improve your powers and get to know other Gyfted kids."

"You're fortunate to have such a powerful Gyft," Mom went on. "But spontaneous combustion is also quite volatile. A summer program like this might be just what you need to gain better control over your power."

"Of course, it's your choice, son," Dad assured me. "It says in the brochure that the program doesn't start for another week. We'll leave the decision up to you."

I stared at the brochure, uncertainty drifting through my mind. Did I really want to spend my next two months at some kind of training camp for kids with superpowers?

But it wasn't just that. Everything about the Gyfted & Talented program just seemed . . . off. The unexplained notes appearing out of nowhere. The warning that had come moments before the substitute librarian had tried to rip my head off. And what about that line about saving the world? What if that wasn't just a figure of speech?

Whatever was going on, I had a hunch there was a lot the brochure wasn't telling us.

5

"Next up—Dragon's Breath!" Milton pointed toward a roller coaster that looped and twisted around a huge green dragon. "And it even shoots real fire out of its mouth! We should hurry before the line gets any longer!"

It was the third day of the summer break, and we were at AwesomeWorld, the new amusement park Milton wouldn't stop talking about. He'd been dragging us around the park all morning, from one ride to another—each with a more intimidating name than the last. The Steamroller, Death-Trap, the Barfonator.

"What's the big rush?" Sophie called after him.

Milton turned back to face us, huffing to catch his breath. "Gotta cram as much fun into the summer before leaving for Gyfted and Talented."

There was no telling whether Milton's forged invitation

slip would get him in, but he wasn't going to let that stop him from trying. I wasn't nearly so certain about the idea. The night before, I'd gone online to find out more, but that had turned up nothing. There wasn't a single website that traced back to Gyfted & Talented.

It was like it didn't exist at all.

The entire program was shrouded in mystery. All I had to go on were the materials that had popped up out of no-where. The strange notes, the letter, the brochure. And those weren't exactly crammed with informative details. I still had no idea where Gyfted & Talented was located, or how many kids were attending, or what we would do once we got there. There wasn't even a sign-up form.

Not that my parents seemed to mind. They'd built their careers around secrecy. The fact that it was impossible to find any information about Gyfted & Talented only made it seem more legitimate to them.

"Do you mind if we take a break first?" Sophie asked. "I'm still woozy from the Barfonator."

"Fine." Milton sighed. "I'm gonna check out the gift shop. Be right back!"

As Milton jogged off, I turned to Sophie. "Have you thought any more about Gyfted and Talented?"

"It sounds like fun," Sophie replied. "And it beats sitting around with nothing to do."

I shrugged. "I was kind of looking forward to sitting around with nothing to do."

"But you're going? Right?"

"I don't know. The whole thing seems a little suspicious.

If Gyfted and Talented is so great, why can't I find it on Google?"

"They're probably just good at keeping it under wraps. So many Gyfted kids together in one place, they have to be secretive."

"What's your dad say about it?"

Annoyance flickered in Sophie's eyes. "He probably wouldn't even *notice* if I went away for two months."

I was immediately sorry for bringing Captain Justice into the conversation. The reality show was taking up all his time these days. Luckily, Sophie had other things to focus on. Like convincing me to come with her to Gyfted & Talented. She pointed to a pink kiosk nearby.

"I'm getting cotton candy," she said. "If I split it with you, will you at least *think* about going?"

Her blue-gray eyes set on me expectantly as a half smile formed on her lips.

I was about to take Sophie up on the offer when I heard a scream.

"The sky!" someone behind me yelled. "Something's falling!"

Looking up, I saw a blazing red object scorching across the blue sky. My first thought was a crashing airplane, but it was way too small. It looked more like a tiny asteroid falling from space. There wasn't a whole lot of time to speculate, though. Whatever it was, the thing was moving fast.

And it was headed right for us.

One moment it was ripping through the sky. And the next it was crashing into AwesomeWorld. On its way, it grazed the sign for Corny Cahill's Corn Dog Emporium, a four-story-tall fake corn dog. The sign erupted into flames, and the object slammed into the pavement below.

As far as I could tell, nobody had been hurt. But the crash sent chaos across the entire park. The crowd was a sea of panic. Everyone was screaming. Most of them were making a mad dash for the exits, while some searched desperately for lost friends and loved ones.

Milton appeared next to me, wearing an AwesomeWorld baseball cap and licking an ice cream cone. He was a little too late to have seen the Unidentified Flaming Object but was just in time to witness the pandemonium it had caused.

"I leave for two minutes, and *this* is what happens?" Milton's eyes turned to the flaming sign. "Anyone wanna tell me why an oversized corn dog is on fire?"

"S-something fell from the s-sky." I felt like I was choking on the words. "Asteroid or missile or something."

Questions punctured my thoughts. Where had it come from? And why?

"We've got to put out that fire before it spreads," Sophie said.

She was right. The corn dog was really blazing now, flames reaching high into the air. If we waited for a fire truck, half the park would burn down. No telling how many people could get hurt or killed.

I scanned my surroundings, eyes passing over abandoned

shops and restaurants, kids leaping off a moving carousel and into the arms of their worried parents. And then I saw what I was looking for.

"This way!" I pointed in the direction of the flaming corn dog. "I've got an idea!"

I bolted forward, pushing my way through swarms of people, trying not to get trampled along the way. I came to a stop when I reached a plaza. The space had cleared of people by now, and the only thing standing between me and Corny Cahill's Corn Dog Emporium was a fountain. Ringed by a marble pool, the fountain sent water gushing from a supersized bouquet of stone flowers. Roses, daisies, tulips—each twice the size of my head, squirting a stream of water into the pool.

Ignoring the clearly marked sign that read PLEASE DO NOT PLAY IN THE FOUNTAIN, I leaped over the edge and landed in the knee-deep water.

My friends were looking at me like I was a lunatic.

"Uh . . . Joshua?" Milton said. "I'm not sure this is the best time for a bath."

Pushing his voice out of my mind, I concentrated my thoughts. A swell of energy gained strength inside me, racing through my veins. I splashed across the pool and slammed my hands against the stone flowers.

CRRRR-AAAAAACK!

The explosion of spontaneous combustion knocked me backward into the water. Rising back above the surface, I pushed the wet hair out of my eyes and saw that it had worked. The blast had obliterated the stone bouquet. Instead of a dozen streams pouring out in all directions, the water gushed upward in a single jet from a busted pipe, straight into the air like a geyser.

I rose to my feet, gazing up at the tower of surging water. "Now we just need to find a way to get this water to put out that fire."

"I can help with that." Sophie joined me in the fountain. By the time she got to me, her skin had begun to glow. She plunged her hands forward, palms out, over the busted pipe.

The force of the water would've easily knocked away the hands of a normal person. But Sophie wasn't a normal person. Not at moments like this. She held her hands steadily in place and redirected the water. Instead of straight up, it now shot forward in a long, powerful arc.

Shifting her hands, she aimed the jet of water toward the giant flaming corn dog. The fire was extinguished within minutes. By the time we stepped out of the fountain, the sign had the charred look of a snack that had been left in the oven too long.

"What do you think set the fire?" Milton asked.

"I don't know." I squeezed water out of my soaked shirt, gazing up into the sky. "It was like it came out of nowhere."

"Whatever it was, it landed over there." Sophie pointed to a crater in the concrete beneath the corn dog sign.

We crossed the plaza at a jog, leaving wet footprints to evaporate behind us. I stopped near the edge of the crater and peered inside. The cracked dent in the concrete stretched about ten feet across. And in the center was the

43

object that had caused all the destruction. Except it wasn't a missile, and it didn't look like an asteroid either. It looked sort of like . . .

A silver golf ball.

The little metallic sphere gleamed in the sunlight. Hard to believe something so small could be responsible for so much damage.

"What is it?" Sophie asked.

I shook my head. "No idea."

"First a mutant librarian and now *this*?" Milton stared into the crater, his eyes wide with bewilderment. "Maybe they're connected."

"I don't think so," Sophie said. "The librarian was careful to isolate us so that nobody else was around. This thing hit in the middle of a crowded amusement park."

"And unlike with the librarian, this time there wasn't a warning beforehand," I said. "So I doubt it has anything to do with Gyfted and Talented either."

"Okay, so we've got an alien golf ball that doesn't seem to like corn dogs very much." Milton nodded once. "Makes perfect sense to me."

Our conversation came to a stop when a slot in the silver ball clicked open. A sound buzzed from inside the opening. For several seconds, nothing seemed to be happening. Only the flicker of noise from within the silver object. And then I realized it. Everything had suddenly gotten . . . darker.

Sophie and Milton must've noticed it too, because they were both gazing upward. I did the same, and that was when I saw something impossible to fathom. Darkness was forming above us, like a shadow stretching across the sky. Whatever it was, the effect was caused by the silver object. As the thing whirred, the darkness above formed into three enormous black letters, hanging over everything.

6

There was no time to stick around to see if the alien golf ball spelled out anything else. Sirens were growing louder. And with a busted fountain, a gigantic charred corn dog, and a crater in the concrete next to us, there'd be a lot of explaining to do if we were on the scene when the authorities showed up.

Exiting AwesomeWorld, we headed across the parking lot toward the limo, where Stanley was waiting. Along the way, we passed frightened crowds of people, all of them staring up at the enormous black letters looming in the sky. Climbing into the limo, Sophie grabbed the control box in her seat and turned on the radio. The news was already buzzing with the disturbance. And it wasn't just AwesomeWorld. Reports were coming in from dozens of other locations across the globe, and the list was growing by the minute. It was the same everywhere. A flaming object crashes to Earth. A silver sphere clicks open to project three dark letters across the sky. *VEX*.

Sophie turned the radio off, staring grim-faced at the control in her hand. Each of us knew what it meant. Phineas Vex was back.

All of a sudden, it felt like the air had been sucked out of the limo. Phineas Vex was the billionaire who'd founded VexaCorp Industries, the world's leading supplier of products for the supervillain community. He was also the evil maniac who'd abducted my parents and tried to kill Sophie and Captain Justice.

The vision of Vex flashed across my mind like lightning. It was a face I still saw sometimes when I couldn't sleep at night. The scar running down his cheek. Him glaring at me from across the fiery underground lair with his one good eye.

In the end, we'd managed to escape, while Vex had been buried beneath twenty tons of burning rubble. It had seemed impossible that he could've survived the collapse. And yet his body had never been found.

That was seven months ago. Since then, nobody had seen or heard from Vex.

Until now.

"Why do you think he's doing it?" Milton asked as the limo pulled out of the AwesomeWorld parking lot.

"He's sending out a message." A chill shivered down the length of my spine. "He's letting the world know that he's still out there."

"But if Vex is still alive . . ." Sophie paused, her hands

twisted into a worried knot. "That means we're in serious danger."

I knew she was right. We were the ones who'd thwarted his plans. We were the reason he'd been buried and left for dead. And if he wanted revenge, we were the first ones he'd go after.

I had no idea what any of us would do when that time came. But I did know of one way that we might at least prepare ourselves.

"I've made up my mind about Gyfted and Talented." My jaw clenched as I stared out the window at the dark letters in the sky. "Count me in."

By the time I got home, I expected my parents to be worried sick. But they'd been too preoccupied with work all day to turn on the news. So it was up to me to fill them in on the strange events at AwesomeWorld and the return of Phineas Vex.

"This is just the beginning." Worry was etched across Mom's face. "We'll be hearing from him again soon. And when the time comes, we'll need to be ready."

"Just to be sure, I'll step up the security around the house," Dad said. "And maybe I can upgrade Elliot with some self-defense functions."

Mom shot me a nervous look. Elliot was dangerous enough *without* fighting skills.

"There's one other thing I wanted to tell you," I said. "I've decided I'm going to Gyfted and Talented."

The program was still a complete mystery, but any thought of backing out now was instantly overshadowed by Vex. Just the idea of facing him again made me feel jittery and unprepared, like taking a test I hadn't studied for. Except in this case, getting a bad grade was the least of my worries.

Ever since discovering I had this freaky superpower, the closest thing I'd had to training was the couple of weeks I'd spent reading and rereading a book my parents had given me—*The Handbook for Gyfted Children*. The tips and advice I'd read there might have offered a good introduction, but now I needed to take the next step. And I could only do that at Gyfted & Talented.

Over the next few days, my parents helped me get ready to leave home. Under the heading "What to Bring" in the Gyfted & Talented brochure, it said that everyone attending should pack a duffel bag with clothes, overnight supplies, and essential items.

"I wonder what they mean by 'essential items'?" Mom paused, pursing her lips in thought. "Just to be on the safe side, better pack these." She unzipped my duffel bag and stuffed in mosquito spray, a flashlight, and a fire extinguisher.

The night before leaving for Gyfted & Talented, I took another glance at the invitation. *Be ready early*, it warned. *Very early*. But this did nothing to prepare me for the next morning. It was still dark in my bedroom when Mom shook me awake.

"What time is it?" I mumbled.

"Six," Mom said.

"In the *morning*?"

Her blurred form nodded. "Time to get up, honey."

"Too early. Try back in four hours."

I closed my eyes. Maybe if I just pretended to be asleep, she would leave me alone. Of course, the last time I'd refused to get out of bed, Mom had gone into her lab and gotten a vial of the Instant Fungus formula. A few drops, and my toes had turned the color of spoiled broccoli.

"The bus is waiting," Mom said. "Time to go."

"Fine!" Letting out an angry groan, I staggered out of bed and got dressed.

A little later, my lazy footsteps clomped down the stairs, accompanied by the thump of the duffel bag I was dragging behind me. Mom and Dad greeted me at the front door.

"I'm going to miss you *sooo* much, honey!" Mom said, giving me a huge hug. She squeezed me until I felt like my lungs were about to burst. When she released me, her eyes were glistening with tears.

"Two months is a long time." Dad jostled me by the shoulder. "I hope we recognize you when you get back."

I said goodbye, promising that I would train hard and call at least once a week.

"Just one thing before you go." Dad plucked a small brass bell off a table.

"What's that for?" I asked.

"You'll see." A sly smile formed on Dad's face as he rang the bell.

A moment later, Elliot burst into the entryway. His big eyes glowed from within his metallic, cube-shaped head. He wobbled on paddle feet toward us. In one hand he was holding a coal-black slice of toast.

"I trained him to do that!" Dad said, an obvious note of pride in his voice.

"To do what?" I asked. "Burn toast?"

"Not that! I'm talking about the bell trick. Now whenever he hears a bell, Elliot comes to your service."

"You ringed, sir?" Elliot said.

"Rang," Dad corrected in a gentle voice. "The correct word is 'rang.'"

"Many apologies, siiiiiir. But I do not know the definition of the word 'israng.'"

"No, no—not 'israng.' What I said was—" Dad shook his head, inhaling sharply. "Never mind. The important thing is that it works. I'll bet *Captain Justice's* robot butler doesn't know how to respond to a bell. And I've got lots of upgrades planned. By the time you get back, he'll be like a whole new robot."

"Let's hope so," Mom muttered under her breath.

"I prepared breakfast for you, Mr. Joooshuaakkk!" Elliot handed me the piece of charred toast. "In case you grow huuuungry on the trip."

"Thanks, Elliot." I stuck the burned toast into my duffel bag, zipped it closed, and stepped outside.

A blue and white bus was parked at the curb. The words GYFTED & TALENTED were painted across the side.

Milton was waiting for me to get on. After borrowing my letter and brochure, he'd talked his mom into letting him attend Gyfted & Talented by telling her it was a superhero-themed summer camp. Now he just had to hope that the people running the program were okay with it too.

"Hope this works," he said, gripping his forged invitation.

Once we entered the bus, Milton and I came to a sudden halt. There was nobody in the driver's seat. I figured the driver must've just stepped out for a minute, but as soon as we were both inside, the doors clattered shut behind us and the engine roared to life. The gearshift next to the driver's seat jiggled, and the bus shot forward. Milton and I stumbled down the aisle, nearly losing our footing before we landed in an empty seat.

I thought I heard a man's voice behind me say, "Careful, kids." But when I glanced at the driver's seat, it was still empty. The bus lurched to the right at the end of the street, hopping the curb and barely avoiding a stop sign.

"What do you think's driving this thing?" I asked Milton, gripping the edge of the seat as we jolted over a pothole.

"Who cares? I got on. That's all that matters."

I cast another uncertain glance toward the front of the bus. The empty seat, the steering wheel jolting from one side to the other. Whatever was driving didn't seem to have a very firm grasp of traffic laws. The bus swerved around corners and shot right through the intersection on a yellow light. Luckily, the roads were mostly empty this early in the day.

And that wasn't all that was mostly empty. Glancing around the bus, I saw that only two of the other seats were occupied. Sophie was sitting in one of them. And in the other was a girl I didn't know. She looked about our age, with dark hair and olive skin. I was sure I'd never seen her before, but when our eyes met, she looked at me like she'd known me all my life.

I kept my eyes to myself for the rest of the trip, which turned out not to be very long at all. I'd assumed we would make a lot more stops and cover many more miles before reaching our top-secret destination, but it turned out that Gyfted & Talented was only a short drive from where I lived.

The bus skidded to a halt in the parking lot of a shopping center. Peering out the window, I spotted a bank, a grocery store, and a smoothie shop. And right in front of the bus was a storefront with the sign painted above the door in splashy golden letters:

TANTASTIC

I scratched my head. We were going to spend the next two months training in a tanning salon?

"All right, kids. Everybody out of the bus."

There it was again. The voice I'd heard earlier. Everyone

else must've heard it too, because Milton, Sophie, and the other girl began dragging their luggage to the front. I followed Milton, who paused to stare uncertainly at the vacant driver's seat. Reaching out, he poked his finger into the air in front of the steering wheel.

"Ouch!" cried the voice. "My eye!"

Milton and I took this as our cue to get moving. We hurried out of the bus and into the parking lot, trailed by a stream of angry curses from the driver's seat.

Outside in the cool morning air, I stared up at the sign for Tantastic. Like everything else in the shopping center, it was closed. A thick metal grate covered the front of the store.

"This can't be the right place," Sophie said. "Can it?"

The other girl—the one who'd seemed to know me so well—set down her duffel bag. "It's the right place."

Sophie gave her a skeptical look. "How do you know?"

"I just . . . do."

The girl stared at the storefront expectantly. And sure enough, the metal grate began to rumble upward, revealing the front door behind it.

Tantastic looked like it was open for business.

"So, what do we do now?" Milton asked.

Sophie shrugged. "I guess we find out what kind of tanning options they have."

7

I'm not sure what I expected. Maybe a secret command center. Another monster attack. Instead, it looked like a normal tanning salon. Merchandise was displayed along one wall. Sunscreen, self-tanner, body lotions, sunglasses. In one corner was a tanning bed.

An employee was standing behind a cash register at the front counter. She was tall, with bleached blond hair and a tan that was somewhere between bronze and roasted chicken. Her brown, leathery lips turned into a smile.

"Hiiiiiii!" she said, stretching out the word into at least three syllables. "How can I help you kids today?"

I glanced over at Milton and Sophie. They were both staring back at the woman with their mouths open. Even the other girl—the one who seemed so sure about everything else—looked uncertain.

"First time tanning?" The woman leaned forward on the

counter, her frosted blond hair falling across her orange shoulders like an avalanche. "I can always tell. So let me guess—now that summer's here, you kids want to get your beach bodies looking good, am I right?"

"Er, actually," I stammered, "we were sort of—"

"No need to be embarrassed," she interrupted. "I'm not here to judge your pale, pathetic bodies. Believe me, I didn't always have this perfect tan." She indicated her orangey skin. "I had to *work* to look this good."

"We're not here to get a tan!" I said insistently.

This seemed to get the employee's attention. She stared back at me. For a second or two, the only sound was the repeated *click-click* of her painted fingernail against the counter.

"Well," she said. "If you're not interested in a tan, then why *are* you here?"

Sophie stepped forward and placed the slip of paper onto the counter. "We're here about this." She slid the paper forward.

The woman looked at the paper. The clicking of her fingernails stopped.

"Where did you find this?" she asked.

"It just sort of . . . appeared," Sophie said.

"And what about you three? Did you also receive these notes?"

I nodded and pulled the slip of paper out of my pocket. The dark-haired girl did the same. Milton hesitated. Then he set his jaw and stepped forward to lay his invitation down.

With the four slips in her hand, the woman glided out from behind the counter. A wave of perfume swept past as she crossed the room. When she reached the front door, she pressed a button on the wall. The steel grate began lowering again, blocking any view from outside.

When she turned back around, I felt a jolt of shock run through me. All of a sudden, there was something very different about her.

Her shoulder-length bleached hair had somehow shortened and become a deep auburn color. But that wasn't the only thing that had changed. Her orange tan and chapped lips were gone, replaced by pale, freckled features and bright green eyes.

She looked like a totally different person.

"My name's Brandy," she said, and even her voice had changed. "Sorry to Shift so suddenly. We have to keep up appearances here. That's how I ended up with the beef jerky complexion. Come along. Gavin's waiting for you."

I was having trouble following everything. Did she really just transform into another person? And who was Gavin?

Brandy led us across the salon until we were standing in front of the tanning bed. "This will transport you to headquarters."

"Hold on a second," Milton said. "We're supposed to go to headquarters in . . . a tanning bed?"

"Of course," Brandy said, like it was the most obvious thing in the world. She lifted the top of the tanning bed.

BRANDY

With her ability to look like anyone
she wants, Brandy is a master of disguise.
But when she mysteriously goes missing,
Joshua is left wondering whether
she ever revealed her true self.

"Now . . . only one person can fit inside at a time. Who's first?"

"I'll go," Sophie said.

As she stepped forward, I gave her a surprised look.

"What?" She shrugged, smiling. "I've never taken a ride in a tanning bed before."

Sophie climbed inside and lay flat on her back. I caught one last glimpse of her face before Brandy lowered the top. Pressing a button on the side of the tanning bed caused a faint buzz to grow louder and louder until it filled the room.

I flinched as a panel of the wall opened up, revealing a tunnel. All at once, the tanning bed shot forward, vanishing into the tunnel with a *whoosh*. The sound grew fainter until I couldn't hear anything at all.

"Our headquarters is located a half mile beneath our feet," Brandy explained. "It takes the pod about a minute to get there."

Pod? She must've meant the tanning bed. Before long, I could hear it again from somewhere deep in the tunnel— only this time the sound was growing louder. The pod must've been approaching. A moment later, the tanning bed shot back through the hole in the wall and came to a stop where it had been before.

When Brandy lifted the top, the bed was empty. Sophie was gone.

Milton was the next volunteer. Brandy helped him into the tanning bed, then lowered the top. I could hear his muffled voice from inside.

"Hey, shouldn't there be a seat belt in here? And where do the air bags come out in case of— *WAAAaaaaahhhhh*!"

Milton's scream vanished into the tunnel, along with the tanning bed.

While we waited, I turned to the stranger from the bus. She had a birthmark below her right eye that was shaped exactly like a star.

"Hi," I said. "Have we—"

"Met before?" The girl shook her head. "We haven't."

"Well, my name's Joshua."

A mischievous grin formed on her face. "I know."

I stared at her. First the out-of-control bus without a driver, then the tanning salon employee who could change her appearance, and then a complete stranger who knew my name.

There'd been way too much craziness packed into one morning.

I opened my mouth to ask what the heck was going on, but my voice was drowned out by the sound of the returning pod.

"I'll go next!" the girl volunteered. She fixed her mysterious smile on me for a moment longer, then climbed into the tanning bed.

Once the pod had whooshed out of the room again, I glanced up at Brandy. "The way you transformed back there—that's your power?"

Brandy nodded. "It's called Shifting."

"So that means you can be anyone you want to be?"

"Pretty much," Brandy said in a dull voice.

"That's awesome! The first thing I'd do would be to change myself into someone taller. And stronger. Or maybe I'd impersonate the president for a little while, just to see the looks on people's faces."

Brandy smiled knowingly, like she'd done all that and a lot more. "Shifting can certainly be fun. The unfortunate thing is you spend so much time pretending to be other people, you start to forget who you really are."

I guess we had more in common than I'd thought. Like Brandy, I'd spent a lot of my life pretending to be someone I wasn't. Maybe I couldn't alter my appearance, but I'd been through enough false identities to last a lifetime. *Several* lifetimes, actually.

When the tanning bed reappeared, Brandy said, "Your turn."

I still wasn't 100 percent sure, but after seeing the others go before me, I couldn't back out. I climbed inside the tanning bed and settled onto the soft cushion.

"See you soon." Brandy smiled down at me. Then she lowered the top, and everything went dark.

Something clicked near my head: the sound of the pod locking closed. Next came the humming sound that I'd heard before—except louder now, pulsating all around me.

I waited with my sweating hands clasped by my sides. And then—all at once—everything kicked into motion.

It was like I was on one of the roller coasters back at AwesomeWorld. Except this time I was on my back, sandwiched inside a tanning bed. The pod swayed—first right,

61

then left. The force pulled my body with each turn, but I was too tightly packed inside to slip around.

After following a sharp curve, the pod began to slow down. Just as it seemed to be coming to a stop, an eerie feeling came over me. There was a moment of nothingness.

And that was when the floor dropped away.

My stomach shot up into my throat as I plummeted downward. The pod veered and twisted. All I could do was clench my teeth and wait for it to be over.

When everything finally leveled out and the pod coasted to a stop, I let out a relieved breath. My entire body felt jittery from the ride.

With a sharp click, the top of the tanning bed was unlatched and lifted upward. Light washed into the enclosed space. I blinked, waiting for my vision to adjust. All I could see was the dark silhouette of someone standing above me.

8

"**W**elcome! You must be Joshua!"

The man standing beside the tanning bed was small and stocky, with a stomach that bulged out in front of him. He was mostly bald, but a dense thicket of hair poked out from beneath the collar of his shirt, as if all the hair on his head had migrated downward and eventually settled on his chest.

"My name's Gavin," he said in a gruff voice. "Gavin Garland."

I climbed out of the tanning bed and wobbled in place on unsteady legs. Looking back where I'd just been, I was suddenly overwhelmed with embarrassment. A charred black burn mark stretched across the inside of the tanning bed. It was shaped exactly like my body.

Spontaneous combustion. You never quite know when it's going to kick in.

"S-sorry," I said. "That happens sometimes when I get excited."

"No need to apologize," Gavin said. "The journey to headquarters tends to provoke strong emotions. And strong emotions trigger the powers of Gyfted children. I had to cover my eyes when I opened the pod and saw your friend Sophie inside. She was glowing quite brightly."

The mention of Sophie made me realize that she wasn't there with us. And neither was Milton.

"Excuse me," I said, "but I was just wondering—"

"Where your friends are?" Gavin smiled. "Not to worry. They're in the main room."

I had a lot more questions, but Gavin was already moving at a quick pace. "Come with me," he called without turning around. "We have a busy morning ahead of us."

I jogged to catch up, following Gavin down a twisting corridor. Along the way, I noticed a series of tiny video cameras attached to the ceiling. They swiveled to track me everywhere I went.

Gavin led me through a doorway and into a vast open space. The walls and floor were completely white, stretching out in all directions, making it tough to tell where the floor ended and the walls began. There was nothing else in the room—no furniture, no windows. A sea of white that looked endless, even though I knew it couldn't be.

In the middle of all this were Sophie, Milton, and the weird know-it-all girl. Beside them a guy who looked a couple of years older than the rest of us. There was something oddly familiar about him. He had a confident smile and light brown hair that swept over his forehead.

Gavin gestured to the group. "I believe you already know Sophie and Milton. And this is Miranda." He pointed to the dark-haired girl. She waved, shooting me another mischievous grin.

Next Gavin turned his attention to the older guy.

"And this is nFinity."

That was why he looked so familiar. nFinity was one of the most famous superheroes in the country. Although he was only fifteen, he showed up regularly on YouTube videos and daytime talk shows. He was a regular in the pages of *Super Scoop*, the magazine devoted to superheroes and supervillains. *Super Scoop* covered hard-hitting news like "Which Evildoer Was Spotted Kissing Her Archnemesis in a Nightclub?" or "How Raven Fury Lost Twenty Pounds by Exercising with a Mutant!"

The reason I hadn't recognized nFinity was because he wasn't wearing his usual uniform and mask. Instead, nFinity was sporting a more casual look: a fashionably wrinkled T-shirt and blue jeans.

As we approached the group, I cast a puzzled glance around the enormous room. "Where's everyone else?"

"There is nobody else," Gavin replied. "Gyfted and Talented is a *very* selective program. We only invited the best of the best."

"But . . ." I thought back to the brochure, the images of happy kids sitting around a holographic campfire. "I guess I kind of expected something more like—"

"Summer camp?"

"Well . . . yeah."

"The highly confidential nature of this program requires a certain amount of misleading advertising. The truth is, Gyfted and Talented goes far beyond any ordinary summer camp."

Gavin must've noticed the hesitation that was still gripping me.

"No need for concern." His face formed into an assuring smile. "If you aren't happy here, you're welcome to leave anytime. I only ask that you stick around long enough to find out what we're all about."

I felt a little of my reluctance fall away. "All right."

"Excellent!" Gavin clapped his hairy hands together and ushered me to join the rest of the group. "Now—before we proceed, I believe this would be the best time to dismiss our uninvited guest." Gavin's gaze shifted toward Milton. "I'm terribly sorry, my boy, but this meeting is only for those who've been chosen."

"But—but I had an invitation," Milton stammered.

"Your forgery may have convinced Brandy, but it's not going to work on me. This is an elite group. And unfortunately, Milton, I'm afraid you weren't selected to be a part of it."

Milton's face dropped. His bottom lip quivered. I'd seen him get skipped over when teams were being picked. I'd seen kids tease him and call him names. But I'd never seen him look this devastated before.

"You were able to make it this far," Gavin said. "Which

shows that you're quite clever. But I'm afraid that isn't enough to be a part of this group. Now, if you wouldn't mind waiting in the corridor until we can escort you back to ground level—"

"If he can't join, then I'm not joining either!"

I heard my own voice echoing across the room before I realized that I was the one who'd spoken. Gavin swung around to stare at me. His genial grin dropped away, revealing a sharp glare. For a short, bald man, he could be really intimidating when he wanted.

The look lasted only a second before his features returned to what they'd been before. As he opened his arms, his eyebrows rose over a glowing smile, making him look like an amused uncle.

"It's admirable to see such loyalty for your friend! But I assure you, Milton wouldn't fit in this group. He doesn't possess the same . . . abilities as the rest of you."

My eyes darted over to where Milton was standing. "If Milton leaves, I'm out of here."

Gavin continued smiling, but I couldn't miss the vein throbbing on his forehead. "You know, there are plenty of other Gyfted children out there. Perhaps I should contact one of them instead—"

"I'm not joining either!" Sophie interrupted.

Gavin blinked at her as if she'd just spoken in another language. "What?"

"The only way I'm staying is if they stay." Sophie pointed at Milton and me.

The strain of keeping his smile going seemed to be turning

Gavin's face a shade of purple. "But the boy doesn't have a Gyft! And if he doesn't have a Gyft, that means he's—" Gavin stopped speaking suddenly. His hand clenched into a fist, like he'd just grabbed an idea out of the air beside him. "If he doesn't have a Gyft, he's *just like everyone else*."

Rubbing his stubbly chin with his hairy hand, Gavin paced back and forth in front of us. His feet clicked against the hard white floor.

"I can't believe I didn't think of it sooner." He spoke quietly, mumbling the words as if talking more to himself than us. "This may be precisely what this group needs. Someone ordinary children can relate to. Someone who's just . . . average. Yes, it's perfect!"

Gavin spun around and faced Milton.

"Welcome to Gyfted and Talented, my boy!"

The look of relief on Milton's face was instantaneous. He still didn't know *what* Gyfted & Talented was, but at least he knew he got to be a part of it.

The dark-haired girl—Miranda—spoke up. "Would you mind telling us what Gyfted and Talented *is*?"

"Of course. Perhaps we should all take a seat."

Gavin reached into the front pocket of his shirt and pulled out a black remote control. The device was small, about the size of his thumb (but much less hairy). He pressed a button on the remote, and I heard a whirring noise under my feet. Several panels of the floor opened like trapdoors. Chairs rose into the room, forming a semicircle around our group.

Once we were all seated, Gavin began speaking again.

"With the exception of our friend Milton here, each of you has been selected because you are uniquely Gyfted."

"How'd you find us?" Sophie asked. "I mean . . . how do you know that we're Gyfted in the first place?"

"I had my employees seek you out," Gavin replied.

"Employees?"

"There are many individuals working for me," Gavin said. "You will get to know some of them very well. Others you'll never meet. A few of these employees have the power of Tracking. To put it another way, they can detect the powers of others. They created a database of the Gyfted and their powers. From there, we narrowed it down to only the unique and most talented. And after all of this research, you are the result. You are the chosen."

The phrase echoed in my mind. *You are the chosen.* The same words on the first slip I'd found a week earlier.

Sophie's voice rose up to speak the question that was ringing in my mind. "Chosen for what?"

Gavin paused, his eyes passing over all of us before answering the question.

"You have been chosen," he said, finally, "to form the greatest superhero team of all time."

I gripped the edge of my chair more tightly. He wanted me to become . . . a superhero?

I could think of about a million reasons why this was a crazy idea. Superheroes were supposed to be popular and athletic. I was neither. Not to mention—I was just a kid. Shouldn't you at least be old enough to get a driver's license before you signed up to fight evil?

And then there were my parents. They'd devoted their entire careers to becoming two of the most feared super-villains in the world. If they discovered that I was even *thinking about* joining a team of superheroes, they'd probably ground me for life.

Gavin's voice cut through my thoughts.

"The team will be called the Alliance of the Impossible," he said, holding his hands out in front of him like an imaginary sign. "As a part of the group, you'll have the chance to refine your powers in an environment that's been engineered to help you understand *who* you are and *what* you can do. We'll also put you through an intensive training process. Although, by the way you each handled your tests, I have complete confidence in your abilities—"

"What do you mean *tests*?" I interrupted.

"Before sending out my final invitation, I arranged a minor . . . challenge for each of you. As a way of evaluating your skills."

A flash of realization burst through my mind. The library, the attack . . .

"*You* were the one behind the mutant librarian?" I said, rising from my chair.

"Yes," Gavin admitted. "But keep in mind that I also sent you a warning beforehand."

I recalled the note that we'd found just before the librarian had come after us. *Prepare yourself. You are in danger.*

Some warning.

"The Alliance of the Impossible is a very exclusive

70

group," Gavin explained. "Before allowing you to join, I had to make sure your skills were adequate."

"So you sent a bloodthirsty mutant to attack us?" Sophie said disbelievingly. "That's your idea of a test? What about you?" Sophie turned to face Miranda. "What kind of test did you get?"

"Zombie janitor tried to eat my brain," Miranda said.

Sophie's attention turned to nFinity. "And you?"

nFinity shrugged. "I got a call from my agent."

"But still." Sophie's glare shifted back toward Gavin. "Someone could've gotten hurt."

"I assure you, the attacks were carefully coordinated," Gavin said. "The mutant that attacked you and your friends was well trained *not* to cause any major injuries."

Milton gulped. "Could've fooled me."

"If you think our little tests were upsetting, just wait till you get out there in the real world. You will face ruthless enemies, deadly weapons, and challenges you can't even imagine."

Gavin's words echoed in my mind. He was right. Danger was lurking at the edges of my life, a threat that was far more terrifying than any mutant librarian. Phineas Vex.

"With my help," Gavin said, "you will have the opportunity to sharpen your skills and gain real-world experience that will help you control your Gyfts."

Gavin rose from his chair and paced in front of us. If we joined the Alliance of the Impossible, we would spend the next two months training in the headquarters, where we would eat, sleep, and spend pretty much every spare minute of the summer. There would be plenty of trips aboveground too. And there might even be opportunities to test our skills against real villains. This part caused my stomach to twist into a knot. What if some of those "real villains" included my parents?

. "As I said before, anyone who wishes to leave is welcome to do so at any time. Although it would be a shame to miss out on your chance to become a part of history."

9

When nobody made a move to leave, Gavin said, "Good! We'll be spending the morning getting you measured for your uniforms."

"Uniforms!" Milton looked like he could barely contain his excitement. "Like, real superhero uniforms?"

"That's right. *Real* superhero uniforms." Gavin smiled down at Milton. "Even those of you without any *real* superpowers. I've hired the top uniform designers in the world specifically for this occasion. Trace will be picking them up from their hotel in a little while, won't you, Trace?"

A man's voice spoke. The same voice I'd heard coming from the empty driver's seat on the school bus this morning.

"That's right, boss. I was about to leave."

The air shimmered in front of my eyes, and out of nowhere, a figure took form.

He was maybe thirty, with cropped brown hair. He had the pudgy body of someone who'd spent several years working out and several more letting all his muscle turn to flab.

"This is Trace," Gavin said to us. "I suppose you never had a chance to properly meet."

"One of them properly met my eyeball with his grubby little finger back on the bus." Trace glared at Milton.

"I requested that Trace keep himself invisible this morning," Gavin said. "If any of the wrong people were to see him with you, it might raise suspicions."

"Right," Sophie mumbled. "Because an out-of-control bus without a driver is *way* less suspicious."

"It's very important that my employees are never seen outside headquarters with any of you," Gavin went on.

"Why?" Miranda asked.

"Because there are people out there—dangerous people— who would like to put a stop to what we're trying to do. That's why Brandy is constantly in disguise whenever she's in public. It's the same reason I had Trace deliver our notes to you."

So that was how all those slips of paper had appeared out of nowhere. It was Trace the whole time. We just couldn't see him.

While we were waiting for the designers to arrive, Gavin showed us around more of headquarters. All the rooms looked the same: white floors stretching toward white walls, with enormous white ceilings far above. And everywhere we went, security cameras swiveled to follow our movements.

There was *one* thing that stood out, though. As we passed through yet another identical white room, I glanced to my right and noticed a very long corridor, stretching so far that I could barely make out what was at the end. A black door.

"What's in *there*?" I asked, pointing.

"Oh, that." Gavin's face twitched in a funny way. "That's—nothing. Nothing at all. Let's keep moving."

The others kept moving, but I stayed where I was for a moment longer. I counted at least twenty security cameras between me and the door. Whatever was behind it, there was more to it than Gavin was letting on.

"Joshua?" Gavin's voice echoed across the room. Everyone was looking back at me. "You coming?"

"Be right there," I called, jogging to catch up.

Our next stop was the dining hall, where a steaming breakfast buffet was already waiting for us. Elliot's charred slice of toast had gone uneaten in my duffel bag all morning, and the sight of so much food made me realize how hungry I was.

Once I'd piled my plate to capacity, I took a seat at the end of the long dining table. I'd just sort of assumed that Sophie and Milton would join me. But they'd struck up a conversation with nFinity on their way through the food line, and as they emerged with their trays, the three of them were so caught up chatting with each other that they never once glanced in my direction. Instead, they settled at the other end of the table.

I felt a flash of annoyance toward my friends. A few seconds with nFinity and it was like I didn't exist. Not that I could really blame them. nFinity was famous; he was a superhero. Even without his uniform, he looked like a teen pop star.

"Mind if I sit here?"

Miranda was standing beside me, balancing her tray with one hand and flipping an apple into the air with the other. *Great*, I thought. *First my friends ditch me, and now I get stuck with weird Ms. Know-It-All.*

She snapped the apple out of the air. "Fine, then! I'll sit somewhere else."

Miranda turned to go.

"Wait! I'm sorry. Of course I don't mind if you sit here. I was just . . ." I went quiet all at once, hitting the rewind button in my brain. Something didn't make sense. "Hold on a second—I never said—"

"That you think I'm *weird Ms. Know-It-All*?"

All of a sudden, my chair felt a lot less steady beneath me. I stared up at Miranda as the events of the morning all clicked into place. The knowing look she'd given me on the bus. How she'd been so sure my name was Joshua. Finishing my sentences, as if she knew what I was going to say before I did. "You're a . . . mind reader?"

MIRANDA

Miranda has the Gyft of superpowered
intuition—which means you'd better watch
what you think when she's around.

Miranda set her tray down and dropped into the seat beside me. "Sort of. I don't really *read* minds. It's more like I just . . . skim the surface of people's thoughts. I'm what they call a Senser."

I shook my head, too astounded to respond. It was kind of intimidating to be sitting so close to someone who could peer into my brain as if it were an open window. What if she saw something embarrassing in there? I was definitely going to have to watch what I thought around her.

"That's an amazing Gyft," I managed to say.

"Actually, most of the time it's pretty annoying. When I walk through a crowd, it's like a hundred radio stations playing at once. And believe me, there are a lot of things going on inside people's heads you *don't* want to know. My mom has me working with a private tutor every day to get better at controlling it. Teaching me how to Sense other things."

"What kinds of things?"

"Well, for example, I can tell that nFinity is about to start playing with fire."

I looked to the other end of the long table, where nFinity was seated beside Sophie and Milton. He aimed the palm of his hand down at the sliced bagel in front of him. "On second thought, I'd like that toasted," he said. And from his hand came a six-inch flame that rolled over the surface of the bagel, turning it a golden brown.

"It's like you can read minds *and* see the future," I said.

"It's more like"—Miranda hesitated—"intuition. Like how you might get the feeling that it's about to start raining just from the way it feels outside. My intuition is just a lot sharper than most people's."

Our conversation was interrupted by applause at the other end of the table. Apparently nFinity wasn't done using his Gyft just yet. As he flipped his hand over, the flame gradually shifted so that it resembled a horse galloping across his fingers. Then it transformed again—into a tree, with fluttering branches. A few seconds later, the flame changed shape to become a chubby little man. A miniature version of Gavin. The tiny flaming figure paced from one end of nFinity's hand to the other, waving his arms around frantically in a way that really did remind me of what we'd just witnessed. Sophie and Milton clapped louder with each new trick.

"I could never control my power like that," Sophie said in a voice that was higher, more girlish, than usual.

nFinity shrugged. "I'd be happy to work with you on it. Give you a few tips."

Maybe it was just the light of the flame, but I was pretty sure Sophie was blushing.

I impaled a mound of scrambled eggs with my fork. It was one thing to choose a seat next to nFinity instead of me, but since when did Sophie go around acting like such a fan girl? And just because nFinity was a celebrity didn't mean he had to treat breakfast like his own personal one-man show. I could make a muffin explode, but that didn't mean I was about to go around showing it off to everyone.

Sophie wasn't the only one who was impressed. Milton had been obsessed with superheroes all his life, and he seemed to be admiring nFinity nearly as much as he did Captain Justice.

"Is it true that you captured Blake Buzzard on the same day that you recorded a new album?" Milton asked.

"You're a musician too?" Sophie broke in, her voice squeaking.

I turned away from the conversation, afraid I'd lose my breakfast if I watched any more.

"What's his deal, anyway?" I said under my breath.

"nFinity? He got his break a couple years back," Miranda explained. "Gavin saw a YouTube video of him trying out his Gyft on a tin can. Plucked him out of school, outfitted him in a new uniform, gave him the name nFinity. Now he's a megastar. TV show appearances, magazine profiles, celebrity endorsement deals."

"If he's such a big shot, what's he doing in the basement of a tanning salon with all of us?"

"Since Gavin helped him get his start and paid for his training when he was younger, nFinity's doing it as a favor."

"And what about you? What are you doing here?"

For the first time, the look of certainty vanished from Miranda's eyes. "Ever since I began developing my Gyft, my mom's big goal in life has been to make sure I become a famous superhero. She had me working with private tutors and began signing me up for auditions all over the country."

"Auditions. Like, for school plays and stuff?"

"Not quite. I'm talking about auditions for *Gyfted* kids.

It's how you get gigs showing off your power at competitions. Eventually, if you're lucky, you get discovered."

"Is that what you want?"

Miranda ran a finger across the star-shaped birthmark beneath her eye as if she could wipe it away. "At the beginning, yeah. What kid *doesn't* want to be a superhero, right? But lately, I'm not so sure. My mom pulled me out of school because it was getting in the way of auditions, so I never see any of my friends anymore. And sometimes I feel like I'm living *her* dream, not mine."

Miranda pushed away her tray, rising from her seat.

"Anyway, it's been nice talking to you, Joshua."

"Wait . . . Where're you—"

That was when I noticed Brandy standing in the doorway of the dining hall. "If you'll come with me, I'll show you to your rooms," she said.

We followed Brandy down a hallway that ended in a row of four identical doors. Next to each door was a name.

SOPHIE

MIRANDA

NFINITY

JOSHUA

I noticed right away whose name was missing. Obviously Milton did too. He took a small step backward, staring at the white floor around his feet.

"Unfortunately, due to the . . . unexpectedness of your arrival, we weren't able to prepare a room for you." Brandy placed a hand on Milton's shoulder. "However, we were thinking you and Joshua could bunk up, at least for the time being."

This seemed to perk Milton up a lot. He nodded and so did I.

"Well then." Brandy gestured toward the row of doors. "I believe these rooms should make you feel at home."

Stepping forward, I opened the door to my room. As soon as I saw what was inside, my jaw dropped to the floor.

Brandy really wasn't kidding when she'd said we'd feel right at home. The view beyond the doorway looked exactly like my bedroom.

Every last detail was in place. The faded blue wallpaper, peeling at one corner. The plaid quilt sprawled across my unmade bed. There was even a charred black burn mark where I'd accidentally caused a section of the carpet to spontaneously combust.

I drifted deeper into the room, gaping at my surroundings. The closet was half-open with clothes spilling out onto the floor. (My mom had been bugging me for weeks to put them away.) The windows revealed a view of my own backyard.

But how was any of this possible? What was *my* bedroom doing in an underground facility?

"We wanted you to feel comfortable," Brandy said from the doorway. "We know that it can be difficult to be away from home for so long. So we created replicas of your bedrooms."

"But . . . how?" I asked.

"One of Gavin's other employees is a Senser."

"You mean—like Miranda."

Brandy nodded. "Except much more experienced. By looking into your thoughts, she was able to create near-perfect renderings of your bedrooms."

Great. Another person reading my mind without my knowing it. What else had they discovered while rooting around in my brain? Did they know that my mom kept zombies locked in the basement? Or that my dad had tried to blow up the moon—twice?

"At least I'm finally allowed to see your room," Milton said, looking around. As part of my parents' whole evil-supervillains-who-have-to-hide-their-identities thing, there was a strict rule against visitors, and this included Milton. Even though he lived only a few houses away, he'd never actually been allowed through the front door.

"We had to make a slight modification when we learned that there would be two occupants." Brandy reached under the bed. I was worried she'd come out with a pair of old underwear, but instead, she rolled out a second bed. "You can sleep here, Milton. I hope it meets your specifications."

"It's great!" Milton grinned, his eyes settling on the window that looked out on the backyard. "How'd you get a window in here? I thought we were a half mile underground."

"That isn't a real window," Brandy replied. "And that isn't a real backyard either."

Taking a step toward the window, Milton and I leaned forward until our faces were only a few inches from the surface of the glass. That was when I noticed the tiny pixels forming the landscape of my backyard.

"It's a TV," I said.

"An ultra-high-definition three-dimensional television with motion-capture perspective shift," Brandy corrected. "And the best thing is—if you don't like the view, change it!"

Brandy picked a remote off a side table and pointed it at the high-definition windows. With the press of a button, the scenery outside changed. It was still my backyard, but now it was in the middle of a huge thunderstorm. Gray clouds swirled in the sky. Rain slashed against the shaking branches of trees.

With another click of a button, the view changed again—and again, and again. Next it was a clear night, a full moon shining over nearby rooftops. After that, my backyard disappeared entirely. Suddenly my bedroom window was looking out onto the cratered surface of the moon. Another click and the moon was gone, replaced by a landscape of snow-topped mountains, a stone castle nestled into the side of a faraway cliff.

"There are hundreds of possibilities," Brandy said. "All with the push of a button."

"Awesome!" Milton said. "Do the windows get cable?"

Brandy chuckled. "Yes, you can watch regular TV too."

Milton looked like he was about to kick back and start channel surfing, but Brandy had something else in mind.

"We'll have your luggage delivered in a few minutes," she said. "But for now, if you'll follow me out into the main facility, I believe the Smicks should be arriving soon."

"Who're the Smicks?" I asked.

"The uniform designers. And just a word of warning . . . When you meet them, try not to stare."

"Stare? Why would we stare?"

Brandy looked at me like she knew something I didn't. I was getting used to that look. "You'll see."

10

Brandy called everyone together except nFinity. Since he already had a uniform, there was no need for him to meet with the Smicks (although I got the impression that Sophie would've liked to have him along). As Brandy led us back through the series of all-white hallways and chambers, I looked up at the tiny surveillance cameras, wondering who was watching on the other end.

When we reached the main room, Gavin was already there, talking with the Smicks. The designers were huddled closely together—weirdly close, actually. Almost like the three of them were taking part in a big group hug.

It wasn't until they turned to face us that I realized the Smicks weren't hugging. They were . . . *connected*.

Our uniform designers were Siamese triplets.

Despite Brandy's warning, I couldn't help staring. Each

was connected to the other by the torso, meaning that they had three heads, two arms, and six legs—all stretched across three bodies. They were wearing a customized black turtleneck sweater that fit all three of them. And they weren't identical. In fact, they looked about as different from each other as possible.

Gavin introduced us.

There was Helmi, the tall, slender woman who was at the left end of the trio. Like the other two, she looked around fifty years old. She had a long, arched nose that seemed to sniff down at everything and everyone (including her two siblings) with disdain.

On the far right was Gertrude, a short, plump woman with puckered lips and a nose that looked like a turnip.

And between them was Mortimer. He wasn't quite as tall and slender as Helmi, and not quite as short and fat as Gertrude. He had big, bulging eyes that darted from left to right, as if he were never quite sure where to look.

"I *loooove* what you've done with the place," Gertrude droned to Gavin, glancing calmly at the blank white walls around her.

"Less is more," added Helmi. "In this case, *much* less."

"But we're not here for your underground facility," Mortimer said.

"So?" Helmi looked down her long nose at Gavin. "Where are they?"

Gavin pointed to us. "Ladies and gentleman, I present to you . . . the Alliance of the Impossible!"

As if they hadn't noticed us standing beside them all this time, the triplets turned to look in our direction. Three heads, six eyes, all coldly gazing our way.

"Them?" Helmi sniffed.

"Goodness!" Gertrude said. "They get younger every time, don't they, Gavin?"

"They might be young," Gavin said, "but they're all supremely talented. The best in the country."

After a long pause, Mortimer finally spoke: "I suppose we can come up with *something*."

"It would be a shame for future generations of superheroes to go out looking like *that*." Helmi curled her lip at the clothes we were wearing.

Gavin led the Smicks to the room where the designers would do their work. The triplets moved surprisingly well, considering all six of their legs had to walk at the same speed. In order to pass through the doorway, they turned sideways and scuttled inside one at a time.

"The Smicks will be seeing each of you individually," Gavin told us. "First up is Miranda."

I felt a twinge of pity for her. The Smicks took intimidation to a whole new level.

"Don't worry about them," Brandy said. "They were like that with me too."

"What do you mean?" Sophie asked.

Trace stepped forward, his eyes flicking down toward Sophie dismissively. "You're not the first team of superheroes Gavin's put together, kid."

"*You* used to be in a superhero group?"

"Hey, don't act so surprised," Trace said. "I used to be pretty good back in the day. We both were."

"That was a long time ago." Brandy touched the ends of her short auburn hair, looking away.

"Brandy? Trace? Come help set up the designers' room," Gavin called.

I wanted to know more. But it would have to wait.

Sophie invited us into her bedroom to hang out while we waited for our sessions with the Smicks.

It looked exactly the way I remembered. A desk in the corner was piled with books; clothes were draped over the bedpost. On the wall were several framed photographs.

"When'd you take that one?" I asked, pointing to a photo of a volcano spewing lava into the air.

"Spring break," Sophie said. "My dad let me tag along on his work trip when the Abominator triggered a volcano to wipe out the Pacific Northwest. While my dad and Abominator were doing their thing, I got some nice shots of the volcano exploding."

"The last time my mom took me to work, I stared at a filing cabinet for three hours," Milton grumbled.

"I had to use a zoom lens to get enough detail," Sophie went on, suddenly caught up in her own excitement. She always got this way when she talked about photography. "But if I zoomed too much, the display would get too shaky. So I had to find just the right balance. Plus, the

Abominator's mutants were rampaging the building next door, which made it kind of tough to concentrate."

"It's really nice," I said, taking another step into the room.

"You should see the photos my mom used to take. Before . . ." Sophie's voice trailed away, but I couldn't help filling in the blank in my mind. *Before she died* . . .

Sophie's mom had been killed in a car bomb explosion. And the bomb had been planted by Phineas Vex. Just one more reason to worry that Vex was still alive, still out there somewhere. The thought of him put a halt to our conversation. Sophie gazed at her volcano photo, but from the look on her face, her mind was miles away.

Finally, Milton broke the silence.

"So . . . uh—do you guys wanna see what TV channels this window gets?"

He picked up the remote. With the push of a button, the scenery of Sophie's backyard (morning sunlight shining down over the Olympic-sized swimming pool) vanished instantly, replaced by a football field, with players from both teams charging toward us. Milton hit the button before the players could dog-pile Sophie's window. The scene became a marble hall inside an art museum, then a view from the floor of the ocean, with colorful fish weaving between sea anemones, and a blue whale sweeping past in the background.

After flipping through about fifty other scenes, we finally found something normal—a news broadcast.

". . . interrupt your regularly scheduled programming to bring you this breaking news story," said the anchorman.

"Top government officials were stunned by the defacement of three separate landmarks last night."

I drew in a nervous breath. I guess it was just an instinct that came with having supervillains in the family. Anytime something went horribly wrong in the world, the first thing I wondered was where my mom and dad were when it happened.

The anchorman's voice spoke over my thoughts. "The video we're about to show you is bizarre and disturbing. So stay tuned. . . ."

11

Milton, Sophie, and I edged closer to the TV. The anchorman was replaced by a shot of the Grand Canyon. For a split second, I thought the window had switched to another of its scenic views. I was about to ask Milton whether he'd accidentally sat on the remote, when I realized there was something different about the Grand Canyon.

Something *very* different.

"We're taking you live to the Grand Canyon, where unidentified culprits filled the entire canyon with purple Jell-O," the anchorman said. "Reports that the Jell-O was grape-flavored have not yet been confirmed."

My jaw dropped at the sight of the Grand Canyon filled to the brim with purple Jell-O. It looked like the world's biggest dessert bowl.

All of a sudden, the scene switched to another famous sight: Mount Rushmore. But just like the last land-mark, this one had also been vandalized in a very strange way.

"Security personnel at Mount Rushmore were shocked to find that enormous purple mustaches and silly glasses had been painted onto the sculpted faces of the four former presidents," said the anchorman. "And as if that weren't bad enough already, a third incident took place at the famed Hollywood sign."

The view changed again. The four presidents and their cartoonish purple mustaches and glasses were replaced by a shot of the Hollywood sign that loomed in the hills over Los Angeles. Except that most of the letters had been re-moved, and what was left had been rearranged. Now there were only three letters remaining—

LOL

"It's as if whoever did this is laughing at us," said the anchorman. "Out loud."

"Who do you think's responsible?" Milton asked. "Could it be . . ."

There was no need to finish the question. I already knew what Milton was trying to ask.

"I don't think it was my parents," I said. "They've been taking a break from the whole supervillain thing lately."

The anchorman's voice drowned out our conversation. "Reporter Cynthia Gomez had a chance to interview someone who knows more about confronting evil plots than anyone else."

The scene switched to a reporter standing in front of the Jell-O–filled Grand Canyon. Next to her was a man all three of us instantly recognized. His muscles were bulging beneath a tight silver jumpsuit and glittering blue cape. His hair was perfectly styled for the camera.

"Captain Justice!" Milton said, exploding with excitement.

"Dad," Sophie said, sounding far less excited.

"That's right!" Captain Justice boomed, as if he'd heard both of them through the window TV. Gesturing to the purple Jell-O behind him, he said, "I'm here at the scene of a despicable act of criminal vandalism against one of our great nation's greatest landmarks."

"Any idea who might be behind these acts?" asked the reporter.

"That's an excellent question, Cynthia!" When Captain Justice smiled down at her, Cynthia Gomez nearly lost grip of her microphone. "Based on the evidence that's been gathered so far on this case, I can tell you two things with absolute certainty: Whoever did this has a butt. And I plan on kicking it."

The reporter blinked twice. "So . . . um—you don't know the identity of the villain?"

"No," Captain Justice admitted. "Not a clue."

Sophie sank lower in her chair, covering half her face like she could barely watch.

"Maybe we should see what else is on," she said.

"No way!" Milton clutched the remote more tightly.

"So far, nobody's been hurt by these crimes," the reporter said. "What do you think is the motive?"

"To tell you the truth, Cynthia, I don't spend a lot of time contemplating the motives of my enemies." Captain Justice paused for half a second, staring deeply into the camera. "I just focus on stopping them."

"I'm sure that's something all viewers at home can look forward to," said the reporter.

"And another thing viewers can look forward to is the groundbreaking new reality show I'm working on." Captain Justice smiled, showing off a row of perfect, shining teeth. *"Hangin' with Justice,* premiering this summer at eight eastern time, seven central—"

Sophie wrenched the remote out of Milton's hand and pressed a button. The interview vanished, and was replaced with scenery of her own backyard again.

Sophie was next to meet with the Smicks. Milton and I returned to our room, where Milton dropped down on his pull-out bed and clicked through the channels of our window until he found the station we'd been watching earlier. But by now, the news report was over and an old episode of *Are You Smarter Than a Zombie?* was on. After about thirty minutes of mindless entertainment, I'd almost forgotten how weird our current situation was. Except for the fact that we were watching TV on my bedroom window, it felt like a normal summer afternoon. Hanging out with Milton and allowing the time to just slip by.

This illusion of summer was shattered by a knock. Trace appeared.

"Joshua," he said in his usual sneering tone. "The triplets will see you now."

After everything I'd been through over the previous week—getting attacked by a mutant librarian, putting out a giant flaming corn dog, taking a roller-coaster ride in a tanning bed—I'd expected that getting my uniform would be a piece of cake. But after a little time with the Siamese triplets, I was starting to think back fondly on the time I'd spent with the mutant librarian.

I entered the designers' room, gaping at the multicolored tights and discarded capes that were strewn everywhere. A long cart stretched along one wall, stuffed with utility belts and heavy-duty armbands. The floor was littered with helmets and masks. It looked like a bunch of superheroes had just played a big game of strip poker.

The Smicks loomed in the center of all this, glaring at me like I was something that had just fallen off the garbage truck.

"Step forward, please!" Gertrude said.

I must've hesitated a little too long, because Helmi sniffed in an annoyed sort of way. "Well?" She held her long nose high in the air. "What are you waiting for?"

I stumbled forward, muttering an apology.

"The one who *should* be apologizing is the person who put together your outfit," Mortimer said, drawing chuckles from his siblings on either side.

I glanced down at what I was wearing. A T-shirt with shorts and tennis shoes. Pretty much the same thing I wore every day during the summer.

"I picked these clothes," I said.

"In that case, Gavin sent you here just in time," Gertrude drawled.

As soon as I was within reach, the triplets began their examination. They pushed me onto a scale, tugged at my clothing, jabbed me with a ruler.

I felt like a human pincushion. While one triplet poked and prodded me, the other two argued over fabrics and accessories, matching masks with bulky armbands and different-colored boots. Finally, all three designers turned to face me, holding out a bundle of material in their arms.

"Here!" said Gertrude. "Try this on!"

The Smicks pushed me into a dressing room. They closed the door, leaving me alone with the mound of fabric they expected me to try on. A swirl of reds and blacks and grays. It didn't look like nearly enough material to cover my entire body.

When I was done changing, I stared at myself in the mirror for a long time, not quite able to believe the reflection that was staring back at me.

12

"**W**ell?" came Gertrude's voice from outside my locked dressing room. "Are you ready yet?"

"Um . . ." I took another glimpse at my reflection, then quickly looked away. "I think there's been a mistake."

"Why don't you step outside so we can see for ourselves?"

"I don't know. Maybe I should just put my other clothes on."

"Don't be ridiculous! What could possibly be wrong with your uniform?"

"I don't think it's the right size."

This was definitely an understatement. The stretchy material was pulled so tight, I was surprised it was still in one piece. The uniform clung to my legs and arms so closely that I felt like I'd somehow squeezed my entire body into a tube sock.

And it looked even tighter than it felt. Shining black

spandex stretched across my shoulders and chest, decorated with a pattern of vivid red flames. A utility belt was clasped around my waist, matching the gloves and boots that I was wearing. Beneath the belt, I'd been outfitted in a pair of pants that looked like they'd been spray-painted on. Except for the bottom of the pants. Around the ankles, they flared out . . . like bell-bottoms.

I pulled at the spandex around my neck. When I let go, the elastic material snapped painfully against my skin like a rubber band. "Ow!" I cried, rubbing the sore spot on my neck. I looked down longingly at the pile of clothes I'd come in wearing.

When I finally stepped out of the dressing room, the Smicks examined me in silence while I stood there, my hands hanging awkwardly by my sides.

Helmi was the first to speak. "I think . . . it's *perfect*!"

"Some of our best work." Gertrude nodded with confidence.

"D-doesn't it seem," I stuttered, "kind of tight?"

"Tight? Where?"

I looked down at the form-fitting elastic that covered my body. I could see the outline of my ribs poking out through the shining black material.

"Everywhere?"

"Nonsense! That's exactly the way it's supposed to fit!"

"Now, enough debate. We still have one more appointment." Helmi picked up the clipboard again, running a finger down the page. "With . . . Milton."

I felt a stab of pity for Milton, who was back in our room

watching the window, with no idea of what was waiting for him. Not that I could feel *too* sorry for anyone else—not when I was dressed like *this*.

The triplets ushered me into the room next door, where sofas and chairs were arranged beneath a couple of high-definition windows. A ripple of embarrassment ran down the length of my body as I noticed I wasn't alone. Sophie and Miranda were already there. And nFinity must've shown up at some point, because he was seated between them.

And all three were looking right at me.

I could feel every inch of the spandex squeezing me. And it probably didn't help that the tights were giving me the world's worst wedgie.

Let me just say, there's no cool way to cross a room when you're wearing shiny bell-bottomed tights. I took quick steps, listening to the soft squeak of my boots against the floor. Dropping onto the nearest available sofa, I grabbed a cushion and covered as much of myself as possible with it.

That was when I noticed what the others had on. Miranda was wearing a purple vest, covered with pouches and pockets. Under the vest she had on silver tights that clung just as closely as mine did. Sophie's uniform was a bright yellow one-piece that stretched from her neck to the ends of her arms and feet. I could see from the expression on her face that she was just as embarrassed as I was.

"I look like a giant banana," she said, scowling down at the yellow spandex. "The Smicks said it was just tempo-rary. The uniform's supposed to be gold, but they didn't have the right material. So until they get it, I'm stuck with this."

"Don't worry," nFinity said. He was seated on the couch beside Sophie. "Once they put in all the armor and padding, your uniforms are going to look a lot cooler, I promise."

Unlike earlier, nFinity was now in full superhero mode. His uniform was a slick combination of sky blue and red, with his white *n* logo printed on his chest. The elastic material stretched over the contours of his built-in body armor, making him look like an action figure that had come to life.

Of course, it didn't hurt that he was a couple of years older than everyone else in the room. And a lot more famous.

Sophie obviously noticed all these things too. She gazed at nFinity beside her. When his eyes flickered over to her, she glanced away. Her uniform might have been yellow, but her face had just turned a bright shade of red.

A flash of aggravation mixed with all the embarrassment I was feeling. I pulled hard at the material of my uniform and felt it snap against my skin with a quiet *pop*.

A half hour later the door to the designers' room opened and Milton walked in. I'd expected him to be as embarrassed as I'd been, but he actually looked excited.

"Check it out!" he said, showing off his red and silver spandex uniform. "The Smicks designed it to have extra

nFinity

**nFinity has it all—
a red-hot Gyft, awesome endorsement deals,
and major hover skateboarding skills—
so it's no surprise that Joshua's friends get
starstruck whenever he's nearby.**

compartments. Since I don't have any powers, they said I should have more space for accessories and weapons and stuff!"

Milton gestured to the utility belt around his waist and the pockets that were built into his sleeves and pants.

"And you wanna know the best part?" Milton said. "The triplets are planning to have jet-propulsion engines built into the bottoms of my boots, so I'll be able to fly and everything!"

Milton strutted in front of us in his one-piece like a model on the runway. He even did a little twirl to show off the back side (which I didn't think was all that necessary). After twelve years of idolizing superheroes, it must've been a dream come true for Milton to actually dress up like one himself.

Milton went on bragging about his uniform until a panel opened in the wall at the edge of the room.

Gavin appeared in the doorway. His eyes passed across our new uniforms.

"Now that you're finally beginning to look like super-heroes, it's time to start training like superheroes," he said. "Come with me."

We followed Gavin into a room he called the training hall. Like just about everywhere else, the walls, floors, and ceiling were white, with cameras perched in the corners.

"If you're going to succeed in this business," Gavin said, "you're going to need to develop your skills. It's not enough to rely on your Gyfts. Any superhero worth his tights knows that powers are only a small part of the total package. Our training program was created to sharpen your overall skill set—strength, reflexes, acrobatics, hand-to-hand combat, weapons . . ."

The more Gavin spoke, the more unsure I felt. Sports had never really been my thing. During last year's Jump Rope Jamboree, I'd been the one who'd gone to the nurse's office with a mild concussion.

"We'll begin our training with *this*." Gavin pressed a button on his remote. A panel opened in the center of the floor, and a steel box rose up in its place. The box was about ten feet wide, and nearly as tall. In the front was a door that was held closed with a massive padlock.

"Inside this box is a custom-designed technology that's been created specifically for the purpose of testing your strengths and challenging your weaknesses. It's a technology that—"

Gavin stopped talking when a violent burst of noise filled the room. Something had just slammed against the inside of the box. Instinctively, I took a step back. Whatever was in that box sounded dangerous. And angry.

"Not to worry," Gavin said. "The GLOM gets a little peevish in confined spaces."

"Glom?" Sophie repeated.

Another loud clang echoed through the room. The box rocked with the impact. By now, I was hoping Gavin would change his mind and send the thing back where it'd come from. But Gavin had another idea.

"Unlock the box," he said.

The air shimmered, and Trace appeared in the room.

"Uh . . . okay." Trace's voice quavered. Whatever was inside the box, he obviously wasn't too thrilled about letting it out either.

Keys jangling in his hand, Trace fiddled with the padlock holding the door closed. He would've finished the job more quickly, except the box kept shaking and clattering.

When Trace had finally managed to remove the padlock, he swung the door open and jumped sideways with a lot more agility than I'd expected from a guy as pudgy as he was.

Holding my breath, I peered into the box.

13

Inside the steel box was a lump of green goo about the size and shape of a beanbag chair.

I was sure there must be something else in there. Something brutal and deadly that had been making all that noise. But except for the goo, the box was empty.

I scratched my head. Unless the stuff was a giant radioactive booger, I couldn't see what was so dangerous.

"That's *it*?" Milton asked. He sounded almost disappointed that he hadn't been viciously attacked yet.

"You were expecting something else?" Gavin inquired.

"I just thought, with all the banging around and everything, that it would be . . ."

"Deadlier?"

"Well . . ." Milton shrugged. "Yeah."

"Looks aren't everything. What we have here"—Gavin

gestured at the lump of goo—"is state-of-the-art technology. This mucilaginous substance can stretch itself and harden into nearly any form without losing its tensile strength. And its built-in artificial intelligence means that it adapts perfectly to your individual abilities. We've named it GLOM."

"Gelatinous Learning-Oriented Material," Trace explained.

Milton glanced from the GLOM to Gavin and back again in disbelief.

"I can see you're still skeptical," Gavin said. "So I'll tell you what. You can be the first to try it out."

"Me?" Milton's voice rose a note higher than usual. He took another uncertain glance in the direction of the goo.

"No need for concern," Gavin said. "It's quite simple. The technology will customize itself to your skill level."

"Okay. So then—what am I supposed to do?"

"Just approach the box. Slowly. The GLOM will take care of the rest."

I guess Milton wanted to prove himself, because he puffed out his chest, trying to look as confident as possible.

"No big deal," he said, walking toward the box. "I'm not scared of this oversized piece of chewing gum. Nothing I can't— *Yaaarghh!*"

In the blink of an eye, the GLOM sprang forward, transforming from a shapeless lump into something else entirely. A human figure. And not just *any* human figure. It looked just like Milton. Except a whole lot greener.

The GLOM landed in front of Milton. For a second, they stood there, each looking back at the other—as if Milton were staring at a neon green reflection of himself.

And then the GLOM attacked.

In a lightning-fast barrage of movements, the GLOM stomped on Milton's toe, elbowed him in the stomach, and got him into a headlock.

"You see, it's just as I described," Gavin said. "The GLOM has now solidified, using its rubberlike flexibility and sophisticated artificial intelligence to perfectly customize itself to match its opponent's abilities."

The green Milton was now giving a pretty serious noogie to the regular Milton, rubbing its fist into the top of Milton's head.

"You must fight back!" Gavin called out. "How are you ever going to take on some of the world's most dangerous villains if you can't even defend yourself from yourself?"

Milton finally managed to twist away from the GLOM's grasp. He staggered backward, red-faced, while the GLOM watched, hands on its green hips, looking very satisfied with itself.

"Go ahead!" Gavin urged. "Make your attack!"

Milton tried to take Gavin's advice. He lunged forward, flinging his fist wildly. The GLOM ducked, easily dodging the punch. While Milton was still off balance, the replica reared back and kicked him hard in the shin.

"OUCH!" Milton wailed. "This thing fights dirty!"

"What? You expect supervillains to play by the rules? You're just going to have to get better."

GLOM

Gelatinous Learning-Oriented Material,
better known as **GLOM**, may look like a
supersized radioactive booger, but don't get
too close ... unless you want to pick a fight
with a mean green replica.

The GLOM burst forward, swinging hard at Milton's head. Staggering to his side, Milton barely managed to avoid the punch. As he flailed sideways, his elbow connected with the GLOM's midsection. The green replica doubled over. Milton steadied himself, then rose like he was spring-loaded, and landed an uppercut hard against the GLOM's chin.

It took my mind a split second to recognize what my eyes had just seen. Milton's punch had just knocked the GLOM clear off its feet. It landed on its back, hitting the floor with a booming thud.

"Thataway!" Gavin yelled, looking genuinely impressed.

Milton had passed his challenge. The GLOM shifted back into a formless blob again.

nFinity was next. When he got close enough, the GLOM transformed in the blink of an eye from a lump of goo into a perfect green replica of nFinity.

Before his replica could attack, nFinity pointed one hand and released a wave of fire that was far bigger and deadlier than the figures he'd formed that morning at breakfast. But the GLOM must've been fireproof, because it charged right through the flames like they were nothing more than a light breeze.

nFinity switched to a different tactic. He reached over his shoulder and grabbed hold of a long silver rod that was strapped to his back. Pressing a button at the top of the rod caused it to unfold like a giant Swiss Army knife. A deck flipped open at the bottom. Handlebars appeared at the top.

It was a portable hover scooter.

My parents had hover scooters too, but theirs were big, clunky things that took up a whole corner of the garage. nFinity's was slim and compact, its silvery surface reflecting the overhead lights.

With one hand gripping the handlebars and his feet planted on the deck, nFinity launched upward on the hover scooter. From beneath him, the GLOM leaped into the air, barely managing to grab hold of nFinity's ankle.

The two of them soared higher, swerving through the air like a defective bottle rocket. No matter how much nFinity veered and weaved on the scooter, the replica hung on. It climbed nFinity's leg and lunged for the handlebars. As it grabbed hold of the handle, the scooter jolted sideways, barreling straight for the wall. nFinity twisted and kicked a button near his foot. The rod and handlebars snapped loose from the deck. And just like that, nFinity was no longer riding a hover scooter. He was riding a hover *skateboard*.

With his feet firmly planted against the detached deck, nFinity swerved and twisted in the air, just barely avoiding the wall.

The GLOM wasn't so lucky. It was still clutching the handlebars . . . which were still hurtling sideways . . . right toward the wall.

WHAAAM!

A horrible crash echoed through the room. I winced as the GLOM collided with the wall and then collapsed to the ground.

The room burst into applause as nFinity soared above our heads, looking like a professional hover skateboarder. He performed a couple of tricks up there, doing a backflip, grasping the board with one hand and forming loops of flames with the other.

It seemed like he was showing off a little more than necessary. Not that Sophie minded. She clapped the loudest.

Miranda was the next volunteer. The GLOM went after her with a whirlwind of punches and kicks. Miranda countered, flipping backward to avoid a swing to her head. She landed on her feet just as the replica was coming at her with a roundhouse kick. Dropping to her knees, Miranda dodged the kick by less than an inch.

It looked like they were fighting in fast motion. I felt dizzy just watching. Miranda and her replica attacked each other with a stunning display of moves, countermoves, and counter-countermoves. I could see Miranda anticipating what was going to happen before it actually happened. The way she raised her arms to block a punch that hadn't even been thrown yet. Or how she aimed her kick—not at the place where the GLOM was, but at the place where the GLOM would be *the next moment.*

Superpowered intuition. Miranda's Gyft gave her the knowledge of what the replica was going to do before *it* did. She could map out its movements ahead of time and adjust accordingly. No matter how quick or powerful the GLOM was, Miranda was always one step ahead.

After being knocked onto its back for the seventh or eighth time, the GLOM didn't bother to get up. It must've known the fight was hopeless, because it transformed back into a blob of goo rather than face Miranda again.

"How'd you get to be such a great fighter?" I asked once Miranda had left the center of the room and was standing beside me again.

"My mom," she said between deep breaths.

"Your mom can fight like *that*?"

"Not even close. But it was her idea to sign me up for private kickboxing lessons as soon as I could walk."

Sophie was next. She approached the center of the room in her yellow one-piece uniform, a look of intense concentration on her face. By the time the goo transformed, Sophie was already beginning her own transformation— the surface of her skin illuminating like a lightbulb.

Before the replica could lay its green hand on Sophie, she took hold of the steel box the GLOM had arrived in. Cables groaned as she snapped it loose from the floor. In the next instant, Sophie was holding the steel box above her head. It probably outweighed her by five hundred pounds, but Sophie handled the box like it was made of cardboard.

The replica made its move, taking a quick jab at Sophie's midsection. Casually, she stepped aside and let go of the box.

SQUELCH!

The massive steel crate dropped onto the GLOM like a cinder block landing on a spider. When Sophie kicked the box aside, all that was left of the replica was a green, gelatinous skid mark.

Sudden applause echoed through the room. Sophie had

defeated her replica in record time. Meaning there was only one person left to face the GLOM.

Me.

The thought made my heart hammer inside my chest. There was no way I'd do nearly as well against the GLOM as the others.

I tried to think positive. I was going up against my replica, after all. Like fighting myself. How tough could *I* be, right? I was a total wimp.

For a second there, I was actually feeling sort of hopeful. And then I made eye contact with Miranda. She was looking back at me with a silent gaze that was half pity, half fear. Like she'd seen a glimpse of my future. And it wasn't good.

I wanted to ask what she'd seen, but right then a hand came down hard on my shoulder. Trace loomed over me.

"Let's go, kid," he said. "We don't have all day."

Trace shoved me forward. I stumbled into the center of the room, where the GLOM was lying, looking like an extra-large green pancake squished against the floor.

One more step forward was all it took. As if I'd stumbled onto a trigger, the instant my foot touched the ground, the green pancake transformed into a full-scale model of me.

I'd always wondered what it would be like to have an identical twin. Well, now I knew. Except in this case, the twin was green. And it hated my guts.

Before I had a chance to react, the GLOM surged forward and punched me in the stomach. I heaved forward, white-hot pain searing through my body. All the oxygen escaped my lungs instantly. As I struggled to regain my breath, the GLOM grabbed hold of my arm and twisted it with such force that I dropped to my knees.

Gritting my teeth, I focused my mind until I felt a tingling in my fingers and toes, pulsing through my veins. Spontaneous combustion. It was like being plugged into an enormous electrical socket. My entire body charging up, building energy.

A blast of power surged through me. An instant later, the GLOM flew backward.

But the green replica wasn't done yet. It jumped back to its feet and sprinted across the room. Right in my direction.

I flung out my arms to protect myself. A fresh surge of power shot through me.

And then time stopped.

Everything froze in place, as if someone had pressed the pause button on my life. The GLOM was suspended in place, arms outstretched. The others stood, unmoving, at the edge of my vision.

I tried to move, but I was frozen too. It was like being trapped inside my own body. Paralyzed where I stood.

A light began to glow at my fingertips—an orb of illumination that grew brighter, stretching forward like a string that extended from my hand. Unable to control the light, I could only watch as it snaked forward, closer and closer to the GLOM.

The instant that the light made contact with the replica, time started back up again. All at once, everything shifted into motion. A raucous blur of sound and movement. The GLOM was absorbed into an explosion of light. At the same time, I was knocked backward. I was flying through the air. . . .

In the next moment, everything went dark.

14

Where was I?

Opening my eyes, I blinked up at fluorescent panels buzzing overhead and the high-definition windows on the white walls. This wasn't the training hall. Sheets were draped over me. I was in a bed. When I tried to sit up, a hand gently guided me onto my back again.

A woman's voice spoke. "I'm glad to see you're alive."

"Me too," I croaked.

Brandy appeared in my vision. She ran her fingers through her auburn hair, letting out a relieved sigh. And then a second figure pushed into my field of vision, a pudgy silhouette against the harsh lighting. When the person spoke, I recognized the dry tone instantly.

"You're alive," Trace said. From the sound of his voice, he seemed a little disappointed.

"Where am I?" I asked.

"The infirmary," Brandy responded. "You banged your head pretty bad back in the training hall."

"At least you're in a lot better shape than the GLOM," Trace said.

"What d'you mean?"

"Nothing big, really." Trace let out a sarcastic chuckle. "You just vaporized it with your little light show back there, that's all."

Light show. Trace's words sent the memory howling through my mind. Time stopping. The ribbon of light drifting out of my fingertips. Being knocked backward, flying through the air. And then . . .

Nothing.

I'd only experienced that kind of thing once before. Seven months ago, inside the underground lair with Phineas Vex. Time froze, a stream of light snaked through the air. When it touched Vex, he ended up buried under an avalanche of metal.

And both times, it was as if I'd lost control of my power . . . as if my power had been *in control of me*.

"So you saw what happened?" I asked.

"Course I did," Trace said. "That light thingy coming out of your hand—it nearly blinded me. And when we went looking for the remains of the GLOM, there was nothing left. Even plasma cannons leave dust fragments of their victims. But whatever you did . . ." Trace shook his head, exhaling a slow breath. "You destroyed every ounce of the GLOM."

Confusion pitched around inside my head. I'd seen the

GLOM get roasted by fire, crushed by a steel crate, and beaten into submission. And it had always transformed into a new shape afterward without any problem.

"You know how much time and money went into creating that GLOM?" Trace said. "And you come along, showing off for your friends by vaporizing it."

"I didn't mean to," I protested.

Trace gripped the bed railing so tightly that his knuckles were white. "You may think you're a big deal, but I've seen kids like you come and go in this business a million times—"

"That's enough!" Brandy's voice cut him off. "Why don't you tell Gavin that Joshua's awake? I can take care of everything in here."

Huffing angrily, Trace turned to go. I listened to his footsteps clomp across the room.

"Don't worry about him," Brandy said once he was gone. "He's just jealous."

"Jealous?" I asked. "Of what?"

Brandy sighed. "You've got a chance that he'll never get again. A chance to be a superhero."

I thought back on the conversation we'd had earlier. *You're not the first team of superheroes Gavin's put together,* Trace had said.

"That's how we met," Brandy went on. "And that's how we got to know Gavin. He was the one who brought us all together."

"Just like us," I said.

Brandy nodded. "We were in a group called the X-Treme Team," she said. When it was clear that I'd never heard of them, she said, "It was before your time, but for a while, we were quite famous. We were on the front page of newspapers, had endorsement deals. There were even talks of turning us into a Saturday-morning cartoon."

"So what happened?"

"Something horrible." A dark look crossed Brandy's face. Her eyes flickered with memory, and she winced, as if even thinking about it caused her pain. "But that was years ago. And I guess maybe Trace misses it. He used to be a star, you know. And now he's just another of Gavin's employees."

"If he doesn't like it, maybe he should quit." I twisted the sheet in my fist. *I'm sure there are tons of jobs out there for an invisible fatso with a bad attitude.*

"It's not always that simple," Brandy said. "He spent his childhood training to be a superhero. Then he actually *became* one. For years, he traveled around the world, fighting villains and living like a celebrity. There wasn't time left over for school. Then, when everything fell apart, he didn't have anything to fall back on. Being a superhero was all he knew."

I slumped back onto my pillow, my head throbbing. Brandy smoothed my hair away from my sweaty forehead.

"Close your eyes," she said. "You'll feel better soon."

I guess I drifted off soon after that, because the next thing I knew, Brandy was gone. I sat up, glancing around the infirmary. I was alone. The room was darker now, the sun setting in the high-definition window. My head was still aching, but the pain was definitely less severe than it had been earlier.

When the door opened again a few minutes later, Sophie and Milton came rushing into the room.

"Sorry we couldn't come sooner," Sophie said, still wearing her yellow uniform. "Gavin had us in training all day. I'm so glad you're okay. The way you flew across the room . . . it was—"

"Awesome!" Milton broke in. "That was the most amazing thing ever! You must've flown fifty feet! And that explosion of light! One minute, the GLOM was there. And the next . . . *BANG!* It was gone! I couldn't believe you—OUCH!"

Milton jerked sideways as Sophie jabbed him with her elbow. "We came here to check if Joshua is okay," she reminded him in a sharp whisper.

"Oh, right," Milton said. "Are you okay?"

"I'm fine," I said. "So what'd I miss?"

Milton immediately launched into a point-by-point recap. "There was this virtual reality simulator that randomly generates a supervillain, a city, and an evil plot. Then a video on supervillains and their weaknesses. Did you know that a downside of your dad's super-vision goggles is that they limit his peripheral vision?"

I shook my head. Milton went on excitedly.

"And the best part is, the triplets installed jet-propulsion rockets to my shoes!" He raised one foot to show off his boot. "Here, I'll show you how it works."

Sophie cleared her throat. "Are you sure that's a good idea? In case you forgot, the last time you tested out your rocket shoes, you crashed into the wall. And the floor. And the ceiling."

"No need to worry," Milton said. "I'm gonna wear my helmet."

As I watched, he opened a pouch on his utility belt and removed a little silver sphere. "That's a helmet?" I asked.

It was barely the size of a marble. But when Milton pressed a button on his glove, the tiny helmet began to inflate like a balloon.

"The Smicks made this for me too!" Once the helmet had inflated to full size, Milton placed it on his head and fastened the chin strap. He turned to face Sophie. "There. Safety first. *Now* are you satisfied?"

"Not really," Sophie said.

"Good! Now get ready for liftoff." Milton took a wide stance and pressed a button on his glove.

WHOOOOSH!

Like a miniature shoe-shaped rocket, his right foot shot into the air. Unfortunately, he didn't trigger the other jet-boot, so his left foot remained on the ground while his right kicked up wildly, trailed by a blast of steam.

Milton let out a surprised yelp as he levitated crookedly in the air, pulled by one foot while the other dangled.

Fiddling desperately with his glove, Milton attempted to engage the other shoe. But in the chaos of the moment, he must've hit the wrong button, because his helmet began expanding again. It grew until it was about three times the size of his head, making it look like he had an enormous silver Afro.

Milton zigzagged through the air, desperately punching buttons on his glove until he finally engaged the jet engine in his other shoe. That was the good news. The bad news was that the shoes seemed to have a mind of their own. They made him do splits in midair and spun him around like a helicopter.

"Just turn the shoes off!" Sophie called.

"I *caaaaaaan't*!" Milton wailed as he jogged through the air, upside down.

It was only after Milton had performed a few more death-defying aerial acrobatics that he managed to shut down the jet-shoes. He let out a high-pitched scream as he dropped back to the ground. Luckily, he landed headfirst, so his oversized helmet absorbed most of the impact.

"You okay?" Sophie asked. I could see from her expression that it was taking all her willpower to keep from saying, *I told you so.*

Brandy came by a little later to tell Milton and Sophie that the next training exercise was about to start.

"What about me?" I leaned forward in my bed. "When can I start training again?"

"Soon," Brandy said. "Gavin wants to keep you here overnight. Just to be sure you're okay."

I flopped back against the pillow. Spending the night

alone in an infirmary wasn't exactly my idea of a good time. After Milton and Sophie left, the hours passed slowly. The sun gradually lowered in the fake window. A robot in a hairnet came by to drop off a tray of food. When I was through with my meal, the door slid open again. I lifted my tray to hand it back to the robot but instead saw Miranda standing in the doorway.

"They had leftover dessert in the dining hall." She held up a paper plate with a square of chocolate cake on it. "I thought you might want a piece. Extra icing, just the way you like it."

Miranda handed me the plate. Layers of chocolate, piled high with icing. Sometimes there are major benefits to having a Senser around.

"Thanks!" I said, taking a bite. "You know what else I'd really like to do?"

A grin flashed across Miranda's face. "Break out of this infirmary?"

I took another bite. "You read my mind."

15

It was strange walking through headquarters with nobody else around. Our footsteps were the only sounds breaking the silence. Miranda's instinct told her the path that would keep us from being spotted by the security cameras. We wove crookedly down long hallways and tiptoed close to the walls of the rooms we passed through.

Climbing out of bed, I'd been hit by a wave of dizziness. But that had passed and now I felt fine. Better than fine. After so many hours stuck in bed, it was great to be up and moving around.

"I don't think Gavin would want you leaving your room," Miranda whispered.

"What's the big deal?" I said. "It's not like we're doing anything sneaky—"

"Quick—duck!"

Miranda and I both dropped to the ground. The security

camera on the ceiling swiveled past the place where we'd just been standing.

"Okay, so maybe we're being a *little* sneaky," I admitted.

"Ya think?" Miranda giggled.

"Better than being stuck in that infirmary bed."

It was the most fun I'd had in a long time. Visiting the designers' room, we discovered that the Smicks were gone but they'd left their inventory behind. We cracked each other up trying on different masks and capes while Miranda told me crazy stories about the superhero auditions her mom had made her attend while she was growing up.

"During the Florida Supertween Competition, I lost to a girl who wrestled an alligator while wearing an evening gown," she said, rolling her eyes.

Leaving the designers' room behind, we explored other parts of headquarters. Miranda stopped suddenly at the dining hall. Grabbing my elbow, she pointed. Trace had entered from the opposite door and was standing at the freezer. As he removed a tub of ice cream, a chilly electronic voice spoke up from behind him.

"You are not authorized to remove ice cream from the premises."

Trace whirled around. One of the robotic cafeteria workers was standing inches away from him. Two others had stopped their sweeping to watch.

"Oh . . . it's not for me." Trace tried to sound casual. "I'm getting it for—uh . . . someone else."

The robot didn't budge. "I am afraid Mr. Garland strictly forbids you from eating any more ice cream. For dietary reasons."

Trace glanced down at his bulging stomach self-consciously.

"We have brussels sprouts in the kitchen, if you would like to take those instead," the robot suggested.

Trace winced, like the words "brussels sprouts" had caused him physical pain. "No, thanks," he said, stomping out of the dining room.

Once he was gone, the robots went back to their work. But it looked like Trace hadn't given up just yet. A moment after he'd left, I heard the faint sound of footsteps crossing the room. The freezer door seemed to open on its own, and a tub of ice cream came floating out. The tub drifted about halfway across the room before—

WHAP!

With surprising quickness, one of the robots swung a spatula. The tub of ice cream dropped to the floor.

"Hey!" Trace appeared, red-faced and rubbing his sore wrist.

"As I informed you before," the robot droned, raising the spatula threateningly, "you are not authorized to remove ice cream from the premises."

Miranda and I had to cover our mouths to stifle our laughter. Trace stormed out of the room empty-handed.

After turning away from the dining hall, we wandered through a few other rooms, weaving a crooked path across the floor and dodging the cameras we passed. We stumbled to a halt when we found ourselves standing at the end of the long corridor that led to the black door. Two dozen security cameras dotted the ceiling along the way. I felt the same stir of curiosity that I'd experienced the first time I'd seen the door.

"Any idea what's in *there*?" I pointed at the black door.

Miranda shook her head. "I don't Sense anything."

"Maybe we should check it out."

After a long hesitation, Miranda said, "I don't know. Judging by all those cameras, I'm guessing Gavin *really* doesn't want anyone going through that door. Including us."

"You're probably right." I turned to go, but she didn't budge.

"Then again . . ." Miranda's eyes sparkled above her star-shaped birthmark. "Can't hurt to take a closer look, right?"

Getting down the corridor without being spotted took some effort. We edged along one wall, then bolted to the other. We dropped to our hands and knees, crawled forward a few feet, and then rolled to the side. With her kick-boxing skills and her cool uniform, Miranda looked like a superspy. I'm sure I looked way goofier, but I followed her all the same.

When we finally reached the other end of the corridor, I noticed the slim security panel next to the black door. On the front of the panel was a numbered keypad.

"Can you Sense the code?" I asked.

Instead of answering, Miranda concentrated on the security panel. Without removing her gaze, she pressed a five-number combination into the keypad. A green light glowed on the panel, and the door unlocked with a *click*.

Miranda took a breath of relief. "There," she said. "Done."

I shook my head in amazement. "If this whole superhero thing doesn't work out, you can always become a jewel thief."

The two of us stood in front of the door without making a move to open it. A question lurked through my thoughts. What if all the security cameras and the keypad weren't there to keep people out but instead were meant to keep something *in*? I thought of the damage that could be done by a single blob of green goo. Chances were, there were other dangers lurking around here too.

But I didn't want to back down—not after coming all this way. And I supposed Miranda didn't either, because she grabbed the handle and opened the door.

The inside of the room matched the door we'd just opened. It was the opposite of the rest of headquarters. Instead of white on all sides, everything was black—the walls, the floor, the ceiling.

A dim light from the ceiling flickered, giving off just enough hazy glow for us to see a few feet in front of us. An eerie chill gripped me as I stepped into the room. I heard a faint electronic hum and whir.

I moved deeper into the room until I saw what was

making the noise. Some kind of a . . . machine. Wires snaked in and out of the shadows. Light reflected off the edge of an instrument panel.

The electronic hum grew louder. Getting closer to the machine, I recognized another sound. A steady pumping rhythm. Almost like a heart.

Buh-boom. Buh-boom. Buh-boom.

"What d'you think it is?" I whispered, pointing in the direction of the noise.

Miranda shook her head with frustration. "I can't Sense anything. It's like something in this room is blocking me."

I couldn't tell what was beating louder—my heart or the pounding rhythm of the machine. How could a machine block Miranda's Gyft?

Some small part of me wanted to creep closer to the machine—to see what was hidden in that tangle of shadows and wires. But another part of me was suddenly very afraid.

"We should get out of here, Joshua." Miranda's voice shivered. "Now."

I didn't need any more encouragement. I whirled around and staggered through the darkness. Miranda and I stumbled out of the room and pushed the door closed behind us. After the nearly pitch-black room, the white walls and lights burned my eyes.

"Something powerful is in there." Miranda cast a nervous glance toward the black door. "I don't know what it is. But I can tell you, it didn't want us there."

"How is that possible?" I asked. "It's just a machine."

Miranda shrugged. "I don't know. But I don't like it. And I got the weird feeling *it* didn't like us either."

That night, I couldn't stop wondering . . . What was behind the black door? And what other secrets was Gavin hiding from us?

I woke up suddenly the next morning with a light shining in my eyes.

"Time to get up." Gavin was pacing at the foot of my bed. "There's not a moment to waste. You can get dressed in the SUV. We already have your uniform. The triplets customized it since the last time you wore it, so—"

"What's going on?" I mumbled, shielding my eyes from the light. "What time is it?"

"That's not important. You need to get up and into the SUV ASAP. Okay?"

"Where are we going?"

Gavin turned to face me, his eyes burning with intensity.

"New York," he said. "It's time for your first mission."

16

The hover SUV shot straight up a half-mile shaft, traveling from the underground headquarters and through a hatch disguised as a Dumpster. Seconds later, we were bursting into the air. From the window, I watched the tanning salon shrink to the size of a LEGO.

"Where're we going?" Milton asked. Normally he wasn't much of a morning person. But all the excitement of our first mission had him wide awake. "What's the big emergency?"

Gavin turned around in the front seat. "Another landmark is about to be vandalized. Someone spotted a lunatic in a purple and black uniform flying around New York a few minutes ago. They think it's the same guy."

A skeptical frown took form on Sophie's face. "And you want *us* to stop him?"

"No, we're flying to New York to pick up bagels," Trace scoffed.

"I know this is fast," Gavin said. "But it's an opportunity we can't miss. This guy's the top story in the media. If we defeat him, the entire country will know about the Alliance of the Impossible. It's the perfect way to launch the group."

While the SUV soared closer to New York City, I climbed into the back to change into my uniform. Right away, I could see where the Smicks had made their adjustments. The pants no longer flared out like bell-bottoms around the ankles. And the armor around my chest and arms actually made it look like I had some muscle tone that wasn't really there.

But I noticed the biggest change when I put on the mask that the triplets had designed. Black Kevlar molding wrapped around my head, with two holes for my eyes and a gap on the top where my hair poked through in a Mohawk. Catching a glimpse of my reflection, I hardly even recognized myself. I looked like a different person.

Like a superhero.

"Before we arrive, I have something very important for each of you," Gavin said as I was climbing back into my seat. "I would like to give you your names."

"Um . . . ," Milton said. "We sort of already have names, sir."

"I'm not talking about the names your parents gave you. I'm talking about your *new* names. Your identities. Your brands. Your superhero names."

Gavin reached into a bag near his feet and removed several small white envelopes, like what we'd received on the day when we were invited to attend Gyfted & Talented.

"I'd planned to conduct a special ceremony." Gavin handed an envelope to everyone but nFinity. "But due to unforeseen events, we'll have to do this now."

I tore open my envelope. A card slipped out onto my lap.

CONGRATULATIONS!
AS A PART OF YOUR MEMBERSHIP IN
THE ALLIANCE OF THE IMPOSSIBLE
YOUR NEW IDENTITY SHALL HENCEFORTH BE:
FUZE

Most people might have been kind of freaked out to have a new identity handed to them on a piece of paper. But for me, the name was just another in a long list of names that I'd been given over the years.

"What'd they give you?" Milton leaned over to look at my card. He stared at it for a few seconds, his forehead wrinkling. "So your new name is . . . Fuzz?"

"Not Fuzz," I said. *"Fuze."*

"Aha." Milton nodded like he didn't really get it. "They gave me Supersonic. Pretty cool, huh? 'Cause of the rocket shoes. But . . . hey, your name is good too. I mean, Fuzz really rolls off the tongue—"

"I told you—it's *Fuze. F-U-Z-E.* Like the string you light when you want a stick of dynamite to explode."

But Milton was already excitedly comparing his new identity with the others. Miranda had been given the name

Prodigy. nFinity already had a name, and Sophie was Firefly—

"In other words, the worst superhero name ever," she whispered angrily to me.

"What do you mean?" I asked. "Firefly is pretty cool. And it makes sense too. 'Cause of the whole glowing thing."

Sophie shook her head, adjusting her gold mask. "Think about it. The only part of the firefly that actually glows is its backside."

"Okay. And?"

"They might as well just name me Big Insect Butt!"

"Now that you mention it, that's kind of catchy," Milton said. "I can see the headline now. 'The Indestructible Bug Butt Saves the Day!'"

Sophie punched Milton in the shoulder.

"There's New York up ahead!" Gavin pointed at the view of Manhattan in the distance. Skyscrapers rising up over the horizon, glimmering with the first rays of early-morning sunlight. And there in the bay to the south of New York City was the Statue of Liberty. It was a sight I'd seen a million times before in photos and movies.

But never like this.

17

The Statue of Liberty was draped in a giant purple T-shirt. And that wasn't all. Instead of the golden torch that was supposed to be in her hand, she was now holding up an oversized remote control. In her other hand, the statue was gripping a bucket of fried chicken.

I blinked disbelievingly. Someone had turned the Statue of Liberty into an enormous couch potato.

As our SUV hovered closer, I saw someone floating around the statue's head. He was wearing a purple and black uniform with a mask that covered half his face. A jet pack strapped to his back kept him afloat.

"Where are the rest of them?" Sophie stared out at the T-shirt–wearing Statue of Liberty with a look of bafflement in her eyes. "There's no way only one guy did all this. Where are his accomplices?"

Nobody had an answer. The masked villain twisted in the air, noticing us for the first time. His face formed into a strange smile, as though he were pleased to see us.

And then he launched forward, flying out over the bay in the direction of Manhattan.

"Follow him!" Gavin yelled. "Don't let him get away!"

Trace jerked the steering wheel, then slammed his foot on the gas. The SUV spun in the air, following the same trajectory as the escaping villain.

As soon as he reached the southern tip of Manhattan, the villain swooped close to the ground and vanished into the park beneath us. I caught glimpses of him weaving between trees and terrified early-morning joggers.

He appeared again at the edge of the park, rising into the air above the street and shooting between two buildings. Trace twisted the steering wheel, following him into the cavern of skyscrapers.

We lurched from side to side as Trace rocketed through intersections, making sudden turns, barely avoiding the edges of buildings.

We sailed deeper into the city, careful to keep the purple and black villain in our sights. A hot dog vender dove for his life and was buried in an avalanche of spilled buns. The city blurred past the SUV's windows.

Up ahead, I saw Times Square. A crowded jumble of enormous billboards and flashing advertisements. Even this early in the morning, tourists roamed the sidewalks, and yellow cabs jammed the streets.

At Forty-Second Street, the villain skimmed a traffic light. It tipped sideways and crashed into the hood of our SUV. The impact sent us spinning wildly—right into an enormous advertisement for Samwell's potato chips, ten stories off the ground.

Our uniforms' padding protected us. Unfortunately, the SUV wasn't in such good shape. Smoke billowed from the hood, and the back end was wedged into the side of the billboard. We were stuck.

I glanced out the window. There was a platform beneath the billboard we'd crashed into. But beneath that, it was a long drop to the street below.

"Brandy, Trace, and I will see what we can do about our transportation," Gavin said. "The rest of you—do whatever you can to stop that guy."

Suddenly, all of this felt much more real. We were no longer a half mile beneath the earth's surface. And that guy out there wasn't a part of some training procedure. He was an actual supervillain. And he was floating above Times Square, just waiting for us to make a move.

"Don't worry," nFinity said after a long moment had passed. "It always feels like this before facing an enemy. But we're a team. And if we work together, this guy doesn't stand a chance. After all, it's five against one, right—"

nFinity's speech was cut short by a loud *POP*. For a second, I thought the crash must've shaken something loose in my brain, because all of a sudden I was seeing double. There were now *two* supervillains drifting above Times Square. Each looked exactly like the other.

"Make that five against *two*," Milton said.

"Wh-what just happened?" I asked.

Brandy stared at the two identical supervillains, stunned. "No," she whispered. "It . . . it can't be."

Trace turned toward Gavin. All of Trace's usual swagger was gone. He looked like he'd just seen a ghost. "I-it's him, isn't it?" Trace stammered. "He's back?"

"*Who's* back?" Milton asked.

"Fifteen years," Brandy murmured. "I thought he was dead. . . ."

The sound of her voice was absorbed by another blast of noise. Out of nowhere a third supervillain appeared beside the other two—each identical to the others. Two more loud pops, and the number increased again—from three to five.

"Would someone please explain what's going on?" Milton asked.

"He calls himself Multiplier," Gavin said. "He can create copies of himself. And copies of those copies. And—well, you get the idea."

Sophie leaned forward in her seat, staring out the window in bewilderment. "All those other guys who just appeared—they're . . . clones?"

"Exactly."

At least now we knew how he could pull off such huge tasks by himself. He had an unlimited supply of copies working alongside him.

"You've got to capture the original," Gavin said. "If you can do that, it'll eliminate the clones."

"How are we supposed to know which one's the original?" I asked.

"Leave that to me," Miranda said. "I should be able to Sense the real one."

"Good!" Gavin said. "Now get out there and show the world what the Alliance of the Impossible can do!"

The door of the SUV swung open. And before I knew it, I was following the others onto an awning that overlooked Times Square. The giant Samwell's potato chips billboard loomed over us. Below, a crowd had gathered on the street. They were looking up at us like we were just another flashy advertisement. Unfortunately, they weren't the only ones who'd taken an interest in us. Multiplier and his clones were flying in our direction.

The swarm of identical supervillains wove through the air like oversized purple and black insects. The crowd below gasped and then broke into sudden applause. I guess they were under the impression that this was all some kind of free outdoor performance.

"There are five of them and five of us," nFinity said, sounding like the quarterback in a huddle. "That's one for each of us. If someone gets into trouble, call out. Remember—capture the original and that'll take care of the rest. You ready, team?"

"Uh . . . do we have a choice?" Milton asked.

nFinity glanced back at Multiplier and his clones. They were closing in on us quickly. "Not really."

Milton gulped. "Okay, then. Let's do this."

I guessed Milton was eager to start his career as a superhero, because he was the first to make his move. We were at least two hundred feet off the ground, but he leaped off the awning like it was nothing. A second later, his rocket-propulsion boots kicked in. And this time, they actually worked the way they were supposed to.

Milton rocketed straight for the crowd of villains. I watched him, too stunned to do anything else. In his uniform and his jet-shoes, facing down five identical super-villains, Milton looked more heroic than the rest of us combined.

Milton reached into his utility belt, grabbed hold of a silver canister, and tossed it. When the canister popped open, it unleashed a net that tangled around two of the Multipliers. They went tumbling toward the earth.

For a second there, we had an advantage. Five against three. But it didn't last very long. There was a sound like firecrackers going off, and the number of Multipliers increased to seven. Nine if you counted those who were caught in the net.

Either way you added it up, we were in for a tough fight.

"That's the one!" Miranda yelled, pointing. "The original—he's in the middle!"

"I'll see if I can separate him from the rest of the group," nFinity said, pulling out his streamlined hover scooter. He launched into the air, fire rushing out of his hands.

The group of Multipliers dispersed. nFinity followed the middle one as he veered downward, out of sight. Milton soared through the air, chasing after two others.

That left Sophie, Miranda, and me. Without any flying

accessories, we were pinned to the platform, ten stories up. Meanwhile, the Multipliers had regrouped (and had added a few more clones to their ranks while they were at it). Nine purple and black villains drifted in front of us menacingly.

"How is *this* a fair fight?" I asked. "These guys can fly."

"And multiply themselves," Miranda pointed out.

"We've gotta do something to hold them off until nFinity can capture the original," Sophie said.

Glowing underneath her uniform, she plunged her hand into the billboard behind us and ripped away a massive chunk of the plaster wall that the advertisement was glued to.

"Here you go." She handed the section to me.

"Uh . . . thanks." I looked down at the ragged piece of billboard in my hand. Stuck to one side was a picture of a gigantic potato chip. "What do you expect me to do with *this*?"

Sophie sighed, like she was trying to explain algebra to a toddler. "Use your Gyft to supercharge the thing. Then throw it at those goons."

"And you might want to do it soon." Miranda gestured toward the villains, twenty feet away from us. They were launching their attack.

"CHARGE!" screamed one of the clones, surging forward. The rest followed.

Focusing my mind, I shut out the roar of the clones' jet packs. A jolt of energy coursed through my chest and down my arms. I threw the section of plaster material and watched as it arced high into the air, and then—

KA-BOOOOM!

The blast was even bigger than I'd expected. It sent the villains scattering in every direction. Shock waves shook the platform with such force that it snapped loose on one side. The ground beneath my feet suddenly tilted at a dangerous angle. Miranda and I grabbed hold of the railing, but Sophie was already off balance from the explosion. She lost her footing and slid farther and farther toward the edge.

I released my grip and dove after her, stretching out as far as I could, reaching until I grabbed hold of her hand.

For a split second, I had her. Unfortunately, nobody had *me*. Grasping Sophie with one hand, I clawed at the platform with the other, but there was nothing to stop the pull of gravity. My fingers slipped over the platform, and we both tumbled over the side.

18

I knew what was going to happen next. Without a jet pack or hover scooter—without anything to keep me from falling—there was only one possibility.

Splat.

Sophie spiraled downward beside me. At least I wasn't going to die alone.

That was when I caught a glimpse of Captain Justice's face. Relief rushed through my entire body. He'd arrived just in time. Like always. And now we were both saved.

Except something was off.

Captain Justice had a big head, but not *that* big. The face looking out at us was huge. And another thing I noticed . . . he wasn't moving. Beside his face, bright silver letters glittered in the early-morning sunlight.

I read each line of text as I plummeted past it.

Hangin' with Justice
A superheroic new reality series
Premiering this fall

It wasn't Captain Justice. It was a billboard.

The enormous advertisement must've still been under construction, because a few panels were missing. Sections of rope hung down where the rest was being installed.

Reaching out, I grabbed one of the ropes. It lurched, then twisted. Sophie gripped my shoulders, and we slid downward, landing with a crash on a platform at the bottom of the billboard.

I glanced up at the three-story-tall picture of Captain Justice, ropes swaying down from the edges of the advertisement. He hadn't rescued us, but his billboard sure had come in handy.

"Sophie?" I gasped.

Even though we were no longer falling, her arms gripped me tightly. Our faces were only inches apart. Her skin glowed brightly, and the lights from a million flashing advertisements swam in her blue-gray eyes.

"Are you okay?" I asked.

She nodded, speaking in a distant voice. "I am now."

The shock must've worn off a moment later, because Sophie let go of me suddenly and turned away.

"We should . . . uh—help the others," she said quickly. "Looks like Multiplier's cloned himself a few more times."

Sophie was right. There were even more purple and black supervillains than before. But there was something different about the new clones. They looked . . . clumsy. One wobbled unsteadily in the air, as if unsure how his jet pack worked. Another kept bumping into a flashing advertisement like a moth knocking against a lightbulb.

"What's wrong with them?" Sophie asked.

"No idea." I watched as one of the clones accidentally rammed into another, sending them both tumbling toward the ground. "They're less coordinated than the others."

"But why?"

I shook my head. "Maybe clones get less effective over time. Like batteries."

"But then why are some of them still in such good shape?" She pointed to other Multipliers. And it was true. Some of them showed way more skill than others. Three of them were chasing after Milton. Above, Miranda was alone on the billboard platform, Multipliers buzzing around her menacingly.

"We've got to help them," Sophie said.

We decided to split up. She would take the clones below us, and I'd take the ones above. As Sophie hopped around the edge of the awning to make her way to the street, I grabbed hold of the nearest rope. I climbed up the length of the billboard and was almost level with Captain Justice's left nostril when I saw something that nearly made me lose my grip.

One of the Multipliers had spotted me.

My chest thumped with fright. Hanging there, I was easy prey. The villain made a U-turn and streaked through the air in my direction. I braced myself, but the impact never came.

He missed me by about four feet.

"Oooops!" the villain said in a dull voice, soaring past.

I exhaled. The clone was a total klutz.

But he wasn't through with me. Wobbling in the air, he made his unsteady progress back toward me. I could tell right away that he was flying too low to cause any danger. Not that I was safe just yet. It was only a matter of time before some of his clone buddies came along to help out. And they'd have better aim. I wasn't about to just hang there, waiting for them to show up.

If I wanted to survive, I needed to act.

As the villain rocketed beneath me, I released my grip on the rope. For a moment, I was plummeting through the air. Then I landed on his back, slamming into his jet pack.

The clone let out a startled cry. He twisted from side to side, but I held tight—one slip was enough to get burned by the flames shooting out of his pack.

It was kind of like riding a bull in a rodeo. Except in this case, the bull was a dim-witted clone. And instead of being in a rodeo arena, we were flying a hundred feet above Times Square.

The more the clone shook and jolted, the tighter I held on. And after a while, I even figured out how to control his movements. Pulling on the back of his mask made him veer upward. Pushing his head toward the ground caused him to swoop down. And if he tried to resist, all it took was a little jolt of spontaneous combustion to shock him into obedience.

Now that I had my own personal clone transportation system, I was tempted to take a test flight around New York. But I didn't know how much longer the others would hold up against the Multipliers they were fighting. Milton came running out of a tourist shop, trailed closely by a clone in an "I ♥ NY" T-shirt. Miranda was swinging down scaffolding toward ground level, pursued by more clones.

When I spotted nFinity, I knew he was the one in the greatest danger. Overwhelmed by the sheer number of Multipliers teaming up against him, he'd been knocked off his hover scooter and was fighting with five clones in the street. One of them restrained nFinity's arms behind his back, and the others crowded close in a violent mob.

The clone I was riding yelped as I tugged sideways on his mask. We set a course for nFinity. But getting there wouldn't be quite so easy. A couple more Multipliers were trailing us.

We veered to the right, and the two clones followed. When we neared the *Hangin' with Justice* billboard, I directed the clone sideways so that he swiped the billboard, knocking it loose from the building it was stuck to. The two Multipliers behind us tried to swerve out of the way, but it was too late. The Captain Justice billboard smacked them out of the air like an enormous flyswatter.

Steering my clone back toward nFinity, I saw that the situation had only worsened. Even more clones had joined the fight. One of them pulled out a plasma pistol and aimed it right for nFinity's chest.

I had to get to nFinity—*now*.

I gave the clone I was riding a shock and felt an immediate boost in speed. Wind slammed my face. The scenery of Times Square blurred around me.

We were nearly at street level when the villain I was riding decided he'd had enough of being my personal transportation system. Before I had a chance to react, he unlatched himself from the straps of his jet pack and dropped away.

As the clone slipped out of my grip, I was left holding his jet pack. Except, without any way to control it, it wasn't much of a jet pack at all. The rocket propulsion sputtered out. I still had so much momentum that I continued racing forward—even without jets roaring beneath me. Like a bowling ball, I slammed right through the pack of Multipliers.

My sudden intrusion caused enough of a disturbance for nFinity to free himself. The moment before I smashed into the pavement, he grabbed hold of the jet pack, slid his arms through the straps, and activated the propulsion engine. With a sudden jolt upward, we were flying again.

Instead of clutching the clone's back, I'd hitched a ride on nFinity.

We rose into the air, high enough for me to survey the scene below. It looked like the rest of the team had gained the upper hand. An entire group of Multipliers was sprawled out, unconscious, in the street beside a glowing

Sophie. Milton had captured a couple more in another of his nets.

Just as the police moved in to make arrests, the clones began to vanish. One moment they were there, and the next . . . gone. Except for one: a single purple and black supervillain, racing through an intersection. Behind him, Miranda was in pursuit.

"Over there." I pointed at the chase. "That must be the real Multiplier. All the other clones just disappeared."

I held tight as nFinity steered in their direction, flying past a bright array of advertisements, and twisting between buildings. But by the time we reached Miranda, Multiplier was gone.

nFinity and I landed on the sidewalk beside Miranda. Even after releasing my grip and standing on steady ground, my legs still felt wobbly and my heart hammered in my chest.

"What happened?" nFinity asked.

"I lost him." Miranda stomped a foot against the sidewalk. "He escaped in a cab."

I looked out at the street, a flood of yellow cabs streaming away from us. When I turned back the way we'd come, I flinched. Hordes of people were rushing in our direction. This time, it wasn't Multiplier and his clones, though. These people had microphones and cameras.

We were being mobbed by journalists.

I assumed they wanted to talk to nFinity. He was the famous one, after all. But as the journalists neared, it looked like they had someone else in their sights.

Me.

A video camera jammed into my shoulder. A microphone nudged my nose. Questions came at me from all directions.

"Where'd you learn to ride a clone on a jet pack?"

"Who designed your uniform?"

"You saved nFinity's life. How does that feel?"

The light of a camera's flash blinded me. I looked to nFinity and Miranda for help, but they'd vanished in the crowd.

One of the journalists pushed in close, holding out a tape recorder. "Who are you?" she yelled. "What's your name?"

Cameras hovered around me like unblinking eyes. All of a sudden, my uniform felt like it was squeezing me too tightly, suffocating me. I needed to catch my breath, I needed to sit down, I needed to get away from all this. But there was nowhere to go. Reporters were everywhere, crowding me on all sides.

The question came again, from more of the journalists this time. Everyone wanted to know—

"What's your name?"

My memory skipped back to the ride over here in the hover SUV. Opening the little white envelope, pulling out a card. But I was so flustered, the only name that I could remember was "Fuzz."

That couldn't be the name. Could it?

A microphone poked me in the chin. "My name is . . ." The word "Fuzz" kept repeating itself in my head, like a demented pep rally cheer.

Fuzz, Fuzz, Fuzz . . .

"I—uh . . . I don't *have* a name."

This drew some curious looks from the crowd. Luckily, Gavin stepped in before I had to face any further questioning.

"We're gonna have to put the questions on hold for now, folks," he said. "If you'd like to request an interview with this fantastic new superheroic talent, please feel free to contact me."

Like magic, Gavin produced a stack of business cards from behind his back. He tossed them out to the journalists and cameramen as if throwing crumbs to a cluster of pigeons. During the scramble to pick up his cards, Gavin led me firmly out of the group toward the SUV that was hovering a few feet away.

"I don't know what happened back there," I said. "I'm—I'm sorry."

"Sorry for what?" Gavin glanced down at me, a knowing grin flashing across his face. "You're about to be the most famous kid on earth."

19

Everyone else was already in the SUV by the time I rushed inside.

"Somehow I just *knew* it was Multiplier," Miranda said as we lifted off. "I mean—the *real* Multiplier. His thoughts were the most focused. I picked up on the other clones too—but their thoughts were dimmer. With some of them, I could barely Sense their thoughts at all. Each clone he created was weaker than the previous one."

"It's like making a copy of a copy of a copy," Brandy said. "Each new version is a little farther from the original. A little more faded. A few extra flaws."

So that was why some of the clones had been clumsier and stupider than others. Multiplier only cloned himself the first time. After that, every new clone was a weaker copy of the previous clone.

When we arrived back at headquarters, Gavin pulled me apart from the others. "Come with me. We've gotta get you ready for the first round of solo interviews."

"You mean—like . . . alone?" I asked.

Trace appeared out of midair beside us, snickering. "That's usually what 'solo' means."

"Can't we bring in the others? We're a team, right?"

"There'll be time for them later," Gavin said. "Right now, I've got a hundred journalists dying to talk to you one-on-one. Just look at the press you're getting."

Gavin reached into his jacket and pulled out a tablet computer. Tapping the touch screen, he flipped the tablet around and showed me the website for the *New York Gazette*. In the center of the screen was a photo of me in my uniform, riding across Times Square on the back of a clone in a jet pack.

Above the photo was a headline:

Who Is the Nameless Hero?

"Every newspaper, blog, magazine, and TV show in the world is talking about you," Gavin said. "And they're all calling you the same thing."

"The Nameless Hero." The words sounded bizarre coming out of my mouth.

"It's got a nice ring to it, huh?" Gavin smiled down at me. "Creates an aura of mystery around you. The media loves that kind of junk! And now we've gotta give them what they want. *You*."

My stomach performed a somersault. My whole life, I'd

done everything possible to *avoid* attention. Living under a secret identity, changing towns every couple of years. The last time I'd had to give a class presentation, I'd been so nervous that I'd nearly thrown up on the overhead projector. And now I was getting that same queasy feeling again. Except this time, it was like I was being asked to do my class presentation in front of the entire world. *While* wearing spandex tights.

I wondered whether my utility belt came with a barf bag.

"Don't sweat it so much, kid." Gavin patted me on the shoulder. "You handled a supervillain and his clones. I think you'll be able to deal with a journalist or two."

"Yeah, but at least I could use my spontaneous combustion on the supervillain," I muttered.

Gavin led me into the conference room, instructing me to take a seat. "I'll bring in the first interview," he said.

On his way out the door, Gavin nearly collided with Milton and Sophie. Milton was carrying a tray of food, and Sophie waved at me through the doorway. I tried to wave back, but Gavin blocked my view.

"Hey, Gavin," I heard Sophie say. "Is it all right if we talk to Joshua for a few minutes?"

"I'm afraid the Nameless Hero doesn't have time right now," Gavin said.

Milton looked confused. "The Nameless *What*?"

"We're going to have journalists visiting headquarters soon," Gavin said in a strict tone. "It's important that you stick to the official names. Got it?"

"I thought Joshua's official name was Fuzz."

"We'll be more careful," Sophie said quickly. "Do you mind if we just drop off this food for him, then?"

Gavin wasn't budging. "The Nameless Hero will be receiving a private meal," he said.

"A private meal?"

"Now you really must be going. We have a busy schedule."

Gavin ushered Milton and Sophie away from the conference room.

While I waited, Brandy delivered my meal on a silver platter. Gavin's Sensers must've done some more digging around in my brain, because Brandy brought the same meal my parents let me have for my birthday every year. A hamburger with no tomato, extra pickles, and Swiss cheese grilled into both buns, along with a side of extra-crispy french fries.

"Gavin wanted to reward you for your outstanding performance this morning," Brandy said, setting down the silver platter in front of me.

My mouth watered. Maybe if I concentrated really hard, someone would bring out an ice-cold glass of Dr Pepper too.

"I was wondering," I said between bites. "How'd you and Gavin know so much about Multiplier?"

All the color drained from Brandy's face. The corners of her eyes creased with concern. She stared down at the table for a long time before replying.

"You remember how I met Gavin and Trace, right?"

"Sure. You and Trace were in a superhero group that Gavin organized."

"That's right. Well, Multiplier was on the X-Treme Team with us."

I dropped a handful of fries. "So before Multiplier was a supervillain, he was a hero?"

Brandy nodded. "There were four of us. Trace, Multiplier, me, and—one other member."

There was something strange about the way Brandy had left off the last person's name. As if the memory of it were too painful to say out loud.

"We didn't have it nearly as good as you guys," Brandy went on. "No state-of-the-art underground facility for us. We trained in an abandoned airplane hangar in the middle of nowhere. At least until we became famous. Then Gavin moved us into fancy hotels, got us working with private trainers. But the funny thing is, when I look back on it now, it's not the celebrity status that I miss, or the free shopping sprees. It's those early days. The four of us, just hanging out all day, training together."

"Then why'd you guys break up?" I asked.

Brandy sighed. "Once we got famous, things changed. We were young. We didn't know how to handle the attention, the money. Fights would break out in the group. Anger over who got the most media coverage, who landed the best endorsement deal. Multiplier was the worst. He couldn't stand when someone else got more attention than he did. He became violent, unpredictable. And then—"

Brandy paused. She swallowed a sob and looked right at me, her green eyes blazing as she spoke.

"And then Multiplier killed one of us."

It felt like someone had turned down the temperature in the conference room. So that was what had happened to the fourth member of the group. And that was why Brandy couldn't bear to say the name out loud. Because the person had been murdered. And Multiplier was the murderer.

Fighting back tears, Brandy told me the rest of the story. By the time Multiplier's crime had been discovered, he'd vanished. Fallen off the map completely. Gavin and Trace had assumed he was dead. For fifteen years nobody had heard anything from him.

Until today.

Now I understood why Brandy and Trace had acted the way they had when they'd first realized it was him. Like they'd seen a ghost. Multiplier had been missing all those years. And then suddenly he was back with a new look and a new career path.

He'd gone supervillain all the way.

My thoughts scattered at the sound of the door opening. Gavin stepped into the conference room. He was escorting a woman in a blindfold.

20

"Okay, you can take off the blindfold," Gavin said.

Ripping the covering from her eyes, the woman glared at Gavin. She had lurid red hair and matching lipstick. "Was that *really* necessary?" she demanded.

"Can't have you telling your readers where our facility is located, now, can we?"

The woman huffed. "And that roller-coaster ride you put me through?"

Gavin examined his fingernails. "Security measure."

"So where's the kid, Gav?" The woman's voice rose to an aggravated squeak. "After everything you just put me through, he'd better be—"

Whirling away from Gavin, she noticed me for the first time. Her angry expression changed instantly into a broad grin.

"Well, hello! You must be the Nameless Hero!"

I nodded, even though it still felt weird to hear someone refer to me that way.

"It's *so* nice to meet you!" The woman tottered across the room, her high-heeled shoes clicking on the floor. "I'm Tiffany Cosgrove. Staff writer at *Super Scoop* magazine."

My parents despised *Super Scoop*. They said it was full of lies and worthless gossip. And it probably didn't help last year when *Super Scoop* published a cover story on whether my mom's uniform had a "baby bump."

And now here I was—in the same room as a woman who worked for *Super Scoop*, about to conduct an interview.

At least I wasn't alone. Brandy had left, but Gavin was still in the room with us. He plopped into a chair in the corner. Tiffany Cosgrove settled into her own seat, flashing me another bright red smile.

"The way you handled yourself this morning was *very* impressive," she said.

"Oh, thanks," I replied. "It was mostly luck, though."

"Such humility from a boy of such talent! But let's get real. You jumped off a ten-story platform, risking your life to save a member of your group. You landed on the back of Multiplier's clone and used it to fly across Times Square. And *then* you rescued nFinity from getting killed."

Everything she was saying was technically true, but it wasn't like I'd actually *meant* for any of that to happen. I'd been able to save Sophie only because of the ropes hanging from the Captain Justice billboard. I'd had no idea that I could control the clone when I'd jumped onto its back. And when I "rescued" nFinity, I probably should've ended up as a skid mark in the middle of Times Square.

I tried to say all this, but Cosgrove interrupted me with one tap of a red fingernail against the conference table. "A tourist with a camera recorded everything. The video has already gone viral."

I couldn't feel the chair underneath me any longer. According to Tiffany Cosgrove, I was exploding across the Internet as we spoke. Within minutes of the fight in Times Square, the Nameless Hero had become the most common search term on Google. There was already a Wikipedia page.

"We're completely scrapping our next issue of *Super Scoop*," Cosgrove went on. "nFinity was going to be on our cover. Now we want *you*."

This was all moving way too fast. The Nameless Hero seemed unreal. A made-up character. How could all this possibly have anything to do with *me*?

"I have a few questions that I think might interest our readers." Cosgrove reached into her handbag and removed a little metallic device that she set down on the table. A tape recorder. "Shall we begin?"

"Uh . . ."

"Excellent." Cosgrove pressed the button on the tape recorder, and a red light signaled that it was on. "So . . . tell me about the moment when you decided you wanted to be in a superhero group. Was it a dream your entire life?"

"Well . . ." My eyes flashed over to the tape recorder.

The glowing red light seemed to be staring back at me. "I never really wanted to be in a superhero group. I always just figured I'd be a normal kid. But everyone's really nice here, and it's been a fun experience so far."

"And how does it feel to be a part of a team that includes nFinity?"

"It's great. He's an amazing superhero."

"So it must be a major thrill to know that you saved his life this morning."

"A thrill? No, I just—"

"But don't you also worry about how you upstaged him? After all, you're younger and less experienced. And yet *you* swooped in to rescue *him* while also single-handedly stopping the villain who's been vandalizing the nation's most precious landmarks. That kind of display would make anyone jealous."

"I don't think nFinity is jealous. And I never meant to—to—" I stuttered to a halt. The light of Cosgrove's tape recorder seemed to be glowing brighter, piercing my vision. "Look, I didn't *single-handedly* do anything. We're a team."

"Of course, of course." Cosgrove winked at me like we'd just shared a secret. "But I want to go back to this power struggle between you and nFinity."

"Power struggle?"

"Are there any hard feelings now that you've clearly grasped the leadership role? And how do you think the others in the group feel? Are they taking sides, forced to choose between you and nFinity?"

The room pressed in on me. I didn't know what to say

anymore. No matter how I answered, Cosgrove would twist my words into knots.

I glanced at Gavin, but he was frantically punching an email into his phone.

"Why don't we move on?" Cosgrove prompted. "During the fight in Times Square, you and the clone you were riding knocked a billboard of Captain Justice off a building. Is it true that you targeted the Captain Justice advertisement as a way of showing that *you're* the hottest new superhero in town—not him?"

"What? No!"

"So then why'd you do it?"

"To get away from the clones that were trailing me!"

"But there are hundreds of advertisements in Times Square. And you just *happened* to knock over the one with Captain Justice's face on it. Seems like a pretty big coincidence to me. You're telling me you didn't even see who was on the billboard when you slammed into it?"

"Well, no—"

Cosgrove tapped on the table with a fingernail again. "So you *knew* it was a Captain Justice billboard? And you knocked it loose anyway?"

"I guess."

"Interesting." Cosgrove clicked the button on the tape recorder, and the red light went out. She dropped the recorder back into her handbag. "I think our readers are going to find the cover story on the Nameless Hero *very* enlightening."

I scratched under my mask, confused. "Is that it?"

163

Cosgrove rose from her seat. "You've done a wonderful job, Nameless. People are going to love seeing you on the cover of *Super Scoop*."

Gavin met Cosgrove at the door to the conference room, the blindfold hanging from one hand. She sighed but didn't protest as Gavin tied it around her eyes. I have to admit, after the way the interview had just gone, I didn't feel too bad when she accidentally bumped into the wall on her way out the door.

That was only the beginning. One by one, blindfolded reporters were led into the room and seated at the table in front of me, where they asked me the same questions again and again.

"How did it feel to save nFinity's life?"

"What's it like being the hottest young superhero on the planet?"

"Are you single?"

After a few hours of this, my brain felt like mashed potatoes. One answer blended into another, until it all began to seem like one big blur. For all I knew, I might've told the reporters what kind of underwear I had on underneath my uniform.

It was late by the time I finally returned to my bedroom, but Milton still wasn't back. After peeling off my mask and uniform, I changed into a T-shirt and shorts before dropping onto my bed. I flipped through the channels on the window until spotting a news report that was broadcasting a familiar scene: Times Square. People running for their lives. Multiplier and his clones buzzing above them like buzzards.

In the middle of all this was a single figure in a shining black uniform with red flames.

The Nameless Hero.

In the uniform and the mask . . . jumping off tall buildings . . . riding on the back of a clone . . . I really *did* look different. Stronger. Older. Heroic.

The recorded footage came to an end, replaced by a live feed of Times Square at night. The sidewalk was jammed with squealing preteen girls. It looked like something between a riot and a slumber party that had gotten out of hand.

"We looooove the Nameless Hero!" one of them screamed. Light from the camera reflected off a mouthful of orthodontic work. "He's sooooo cute!"

I couldn't believe what I was seeing. Girls at school *never* screamed like this about me. Unless you counted the time when I accidentally tripped in the cafeteria and landed face-first in Jenny Lewis's pickle sandwich.

The girls on TV were still having their group panic attack session when there was a rattle in the doorway. A moment later, Milton stepped into the room.

I fumbled with the remote. The squealing girls disappeared from the window, replaced by a view of my backyard at night.

MILTON

Milton loves everything about becoming
a superhero. Even the tights. But what if he
loses his best friend in the process?

"Is that what you've been doing all day?" Milton gave me a skeptical look. "Watching girls scream about how great you are?"

"No," I said. "I was just channel surfing."

Milton looked like he didn't believe me.

"Actually, I've been giving interviews all afternoon." I told him about Tiffany Cosgrove and how dull it was being cooped up in a conference room, answering the same questions over and over again.

"Sounds really tough." Milton rolled his eyes.

Ignoring the sarcastic comment, I asked, "So, uh . . . how'd it go in the training hall?"

"They should call it the *torture* hall," Milton muttered.

For the first time, I noticed how exhausted and beaten-up he looked. His uniform was torn. A trickle of blood dripped from a cut on his knee. Whatever they'd done during training, it must've been rougher than in the past.

"Gavin said we would've been defeated today if the Nameless Hero hadn't stepped in to save us. So now he's increasing the difficulty level of our training by about a million. So thanks, Nameless Hero."

Milton made it sound like it was my fault that training was so hard on everyone.

"Not that you would know anything about that," he said. "Since you managed to skip out on training. Again."

I gave Milton a sharp look. "What's *that* supposed to mean?"

Milton tossed his mask at the wall. "It means you sat around in a comfy chair all afternoon while the rest of us were getting our butts kicked all up and down the training hall."

I stood from the bed, suddenly defensive. "It's not like I *wanted* to do all those interviews. Gavin didn't give me any choice."

"Just like you didn't have any choice when it came to eating a private meal instead of going to the dining hall?" Milton's voice grew louder. "Now that you're a celebrity, you think you're too good to eat with everyone else."

"You wanted to be a part of this way more than I ever did. So don't blame me now that—"

"Now that *what*? Now that you're a star? Now that the rest of us get stuck training while you hang out with journalists?" Milton's hands curled into fists. "Now that you can sit around watching all your adoring fans on TV?"

"Listen, Milton . . . I'm sorry."

But he ignored me. Climbing into his bed, Milton turned his back to me. He must've been pretty wiped out, because he started snoring almost instantly.

Early the next morning, a pair of hands shook me roughly awake.

"Time to get up," Trace said. "And make it quick. There isn't much time."

"What happened?" I croaked. Darkness hung over my bedroom. "Did Multiplier attack something else?"

"Worse. You've got publicity to do." Trace snickered.

"Now get dressed in your uniform. Gavin wants to hit the air in fifteen minutes."

On his way out the door, Trace flipped on the light. The sudden brightness burned my eyes, but it didn't seem to have much of an effect on Milton. He went on snoring.

I considered waking him up to apologize about last night, but I'd slept over at his house enough over the years to know that Milton was the heaviest sleeper on the planet. Sasquatch could sit on his head and he wouldn't flinch. So I left Milton snoozing and shut the bedroom door behind me.

21

I felt like I'd stepped into the life of a rock star.

After an hour in the air, the hover SUV descended into New York City. I gazed out the window at the crowd gathered below. There must've been hundreds of people. Kids, mostly. And they'd all come out to see me.

When I opened the door to the SUV, I was met by a chorus of screams. A swarm of paparazzi and preteen girls surged forward, trying to get a better look. Cameras flashed. Handmade signs waved above the crowd:

> Dear Nameless Hero, u r hot!!!
> Me + Nameless Hero = :-)
> NY ♥ NH

This was just a sneak preview. The entire day was a whirlwind of publicity. Appearances on morning shows, interviews with radio DJs, a guest spot on a prime-time TV show. Gavin had every minute mapped out for me.

Everywhere I went, cameras flashed. Crowds screamed my name. Journalists trailed our SUV through the streets of New York. It got so bad that, by the end of the day, Gavin decided to check me into a hotel.

"We can't risk the media trailing us back to head-quarters," he said as we pulled up in front of the Ritz-Carlton.

"*This* is the hotel you picked?" I looked out the window at the fancy entryway.

"You're famous now," Gavin said. "It's time you start living that way. A celebrity like you can't share a room."

"I *like* sharing a room," I said. "Can't Milton stay here too? And Sophie and everybody else?"

"They need to stay at headquarters for training."

"How come I'm not training anymore? All I do is give interviews and get my picture taken."

Gavin sighed, like he'd had this conversation a million times before. "That's a part of the job, Nameless—"

"Nobody else is here. You don't have to call me that."

"You may as well get used to it. People are going to be calling you the Nameless Hero for a long, long time."

I shrugged. "For the summer, at least."

"Yes, well . . ." Gavin cracked his knuckles. "We'll see about that."

I was still wondering what he meant by that last com-ment when the door to the SUV opened. The next thing I knew, I was out on the sidewalk. Hotel employees struggled to keep the mob of fans and photographers away from the hotel entry.

A little girl slipped through security and rushed toward me. She couldn't have been more than eight, with a ponytail and big eyes that looked up at me like I was the most thrilling thing she'd ever seen.

"Nameless Hero!" she exclaimed over the sounds of screaming all around us. "I'm your biggest fan! Will you sign this for me?"

In one hand, the girl had a T-shirt with my face on it. In the other, she gripped a black marker. I still wasn't used to this kind of thing, but the girl looked so excited—I didn't want to disappoint her.

"I'll be glad to." I smiled, taking the marker from her. "What's your name?"

Before she could answer, the girl staggered backward suddenly, pulled away from me by an unseen force. Trace—my invisible bodyguard.

"Wait," I called, waving the girl's marker. "I don't mind—"

"Let's go, Nameless." Gavin guided me forcefully through the doors and into the hotel lobby. "Save the autographs for some other time. We've got an early morning tomorrow."

When I got to my room, my jaw dropped. The place was enormous, with windows looking out on Central Park and the buildings surrounding it. The couches and chairs looked way too expensive for me to sit on. In a separate room, there was a king-sized bed with at least twenty cushions piled on top.

"This is all for *me*?"

I heard a cynical laugh beside Gavin that let me know Trace was in the entryway. "Beats staying a half mile beneath a tanning salon, huh, kid?"

"You know, you didn't have to be so rough with that girl back there," I said to the spot of air where Trace's voice had come from. "I don't mind signing a few autographs."

"Sign one autograph and you'll have to do it for everyone," Trace said. "You'd be out there all night."

"Better than you pushing around eight-year-olds."

Gavin stepped forward. "I know this is an adjustment. We'll work things out soon, I promise. The last couple of days have been hectic, to say the least. Give yourself a break. Order some room service—whatever you want. Enjoy yourself!"

When Gavin and Trace left, I dropped onto a sofa, relieved to be alone at last. I closed my eyes for a few seconds, letting the frantic insanity of the last few days fade from my mind. Then I picked up the phone and dialed zero.

A woman's voice answered immediately. "Front desk. How may I help you?"

"Could I please order room service?"

"Absolutely, sir. What would you like?"

"Uh . . ." I thought about what Gavin had said. *Whatever you want.* I didn't know when I'd have a chance like this again, so why not take advantage of it? "I'd like a . . . pep-peroni and peanut butter pizza, please. Extra cheese. And a—a lobster with ice cream on top."

The voice on the other end of the line let out a surprised squeak. "I apologize, sir, but I believe there may have been a misunderstanding. You want ice cream . . . on your lob-ster?"

"That's right. Chocolate-vanilla swirl, if you have it."

"And pizza with—"

"Pepperoni and peanut butter. Can you make that?"

"Yes, sir, I believe so. But—"

"Great! And what kind of sodas do you have?"

In a slightly annoyed voice, the lady listed off about twelve different types.

"I'll take all of them, please," I said when she was done.

"All of them?"

"Yes, please. I'm the Nameless Hero," I added, in case she needed to know.

There was a long pause, like maybe the lady was trying to decide whether this was a prank call.

"If you'll excuse me," she said, "I'll just have to check with my manager."

I could hear her whispering to someone. When she men-tioned that the order was for the Nameless Hero, there was a sudden rustling on the other end of the line. The manager must've been wrestling the phone away from her, because a second later, a man's deep voice was speaking in my ear.

"I'm terribly sorry for the confusion, Mr. . . . uh—Mr. Hero," he said. "We don't usually receive such . . . creative orders. We'll send the meal up to your room as soon as possible."

While I waited for my room service to arrive, I dialed another number.

My mom answered on the second ring. As soon as I heard her voice, I realized how much I'd missed her and my dad. It'd been only a few days since I'd left home, but with everything that had happened, it felt like I hadn't seen them in weeks.

"Joshua! It's so wonderful to hear from you!" I had to hold the phone away to keep my mom's excited squeal from splitting my eardrum. "How are you? How's camp?"

I'd completely forgotten that my parents still thought I was at Gyfted & Talented summer camp. Here I was, fighting supervillains and staying in a five-star hotel, and all this time, my parents probably imagined me singing campfire songs and using my spontaneous combustion to make s'mores.

Not that I could tell them any different. Something gave me the feeling that they wouldn't like the idea of the *New York Gazette* referring to their son as "the world's hottest new superhero."

"I'm so glad you called, son!" Dad joined the conversation on speakerphone. "Elliot's been asking about you ever since you left. Can you believe it?"

"That's . . . uh—nice." I wasn't sure whether to feel proud or concerned that our defective robot butler missed me.

"He's made huge improvements over the last few days!" Dad went on. "That trick with the bell I showed you—it was just the beginning. By the time you get back, I expect I'll have most of the flaws worked out."

"Hmph," Mom said. She didn't sound convinced.

"So have you heard about this new *superhero* who's getting so much attention right now?" Dad pronounced the word "superhero" with the same tone he might have used to describe a mosquito buzzing around his ear.

"The Nameless Hero," Mom said, sounding even less impressed. "That's exactly what our culture needs. Yet *another* supercelebrity hack."

"I'm sure he's not *that* bad," I said.

"Oh, come *on*!" I could hear the disdain in Dad's voice. "You probably don't have TVs at that camp of yours, but let me tell you—he was on practically every morning show today. Smiling and waving like he's the greatest thing in the world."

"He's just a product being sold to the masses," Mom said.

"I doubt he sees himself that way," I pointed out.

"Probably not," Mom agreed. "After all, he's still so young. I'd say he's about your age."

"*Exactly* my age, actually."

"Huh?" Dad said.

"Never mind." I knocked a couple of satin cushions off the sofa. It was bad enough that Milton was angry with me. Now I had to listen to my parents tell me how awful I was.

So why not quit? There'd been a tiny voice in the corner of my mind asking this question all day. If I dropped out now, I could go back to my old life and still have a chance

176

to enjoy the rest of the summer. No more awkward interviews. No more spandex wedgies.

Maybe quitting really *was* my best option. I was about to bring up this possibility with my parents, but Mom spoke first.

"There's something you should know, Joshua." Her voice dropped away, as if she were considering whether or not to go on. Finally, she said, "There are rumors that Phineas Vex is working on some kind of top-secret project. And he's assembled a team of experts to help him."

"Many of the world's best doctors, scientists, and engineers have been going missing," Dad went on. "We think they're working for Vex now."

I gripped the phone more tightly. "Why? Why would they do that?"

"Vex is very wealthy," Mom said. "And very dangerous. One way or another, he has the ability to make just about anyone work for him."

I looked around my huge hotel room, suddenly aware of how isolated I was. If only Sophie and Milton were with me. But they were hundreds of miles away, hidden deep beneath the earth. Maybe the Nameless Hero had tons of adoring fans, but I'd never felt so alone.

"Here's the strangest part," Dad said. "One scientist who went missing had a tracking chip installed in her wristwatch. It could tell her whereabouts, even after she vanished. And you'll never believe where she ended up."

I held my breath. "Where?"

Before Dad could get the first syllable out, there was a

disturbance on the other end of the line. For a few seconds, it sounded like my parents were playing football with the phone. Then someone new joined the conversation.

"Hellloooo, Joshuaaaak!" came a mangled electronic voice that I recognized immediately.

"Elliot!" I said. "Please—put my parents back on the line. Now!"

"Howzzz summmmer caaaaaamp!"

"It's fine. Now, could you give the phone back to my mom and dad?"

From the sounds coming through the receiver, I could only guess what was happening. I could hear pounding footsteps, a sudden crash. Dad's voice cried out in the distance. "Come back here with that! No, Elliot, don't put the phone in your mou—"

CHOMP!

And just like that, the line went dead.

22

"Let's go, Nameless!" Gavin barked at me. "We're late already!"

I was standing in front of the hotel, rubbing my eyes. I'd been living at the Ritz-Carlton for a week already. The past seven days had gone by in a daze, a dizzying loop of talk shows, journalists, screaming fans . . .

Ever since the events at Times Square, my life had flipped upside down. Crowds formed wherever I went. Plans were already in the works for action figures, a movie, a national tour.

Morning—noon—night . . . it was the Nameless Hero show.

There hadn't even been time to call my parents again. And so whatever my dad had been about to tell me had been left unsaid. Although I'd heard more than enough to make me uneasy. Phineas Vex had a team of experts assisting him on some kind of secret project. But what were they working on? And where had they all disappeared to?

The worst part was not being able to discuss any of this with the rest of the group. Whenever I asked about them, Gavin always gave me the same answer. *They're back at headquarters, training.* With each day that went by, I felt like I was drifting farther away from everyone I'd known before I'd become famous.

But one thing I knew was, I couldn't just quit. Whatever Vex was up to, the Alliance of the Impossible was my best chance to stop him. I just needed to figure out a way to get back into training. . . .

"Hey, kid! Wakey-wakey!"

Trace's brash voice shook me out of my own thoughts. He was invisible in the driver's seat of the SUV. A hotel employee was holding the back door open for me.

"Earth to superhero," Trace teased as I climbed into the backseat. "You look like you're on another planet."

"Sorry." I tugged at the mask that I almost never took off these days. "Still a little sleepy."

"Well, you'd better wake up in time for the commercial shoot. This is a big deal. You don't want to mess it up."

"Commercial shoot?" I asked. "What kind of commercial?"

"The company you're endorsing," Gavin replied. "Very exciting development."

So now I was endorsing a company? Just add it to the list of things nobody bothered to tell me.

I got an even bigger surprise a half hour later when I learned what *kind of* company it was. Trace parked the SUV in front of a studio, and Gavin rushed me between two columns of excited fans and flashing cameras, through the front doors. We were running behind, and there was barely a moment for introductions before the director positioned me in front of a screen.

"Okay, Nameless," he said. "Just act natural. Be yourself."

I glanced up at the cameras that were aimed in my direction, the lighting equipment hovering everywhere. Adults were scattered throughout the studio, all looking back at me.

How was I supposed to act natural when my legs felt like they might give out any second?

"All you need to do is read the cue card out loud." The director pointed to a poster board. My eyes scanned over the lines that I was supposed to recite, but this only made me feel worse.

"You want me to say *that*?" I asked.

The director nodded, taking a spot next to one of the cameras. When he called out "Action!" I knew what was expected of me—not that that made it any easier.

I did my best to swallow my embarrassment, then began to read my lines:

"When I'm not saving the world from supervillains, I spend my time battling pimples." I gulped, sure I was blushing under my mask. "That's why I use Triple-P—Pimple

Prevention Power. Now I don't have to worry about zits while I'm out fighting evil."

"Great job!" called the director.

I took a step toward the door. "Does that mean we're done?"

"Not even close. We still need to shoot a few dozen more takes."

"A few *dozen*?"

"We've got to get this right." The director stood from his chair, pointing at me. "After all, *you're* the new face of Triple-P Advanced Acne Cream. From now on, whenever anyone thinks of unsightly pimples, they'll think of you!"

That was a really nice thought.

So I read the lines again. And again. And so many times after that, I lost count. Each time, my mom's words thudded in my ears a little louder. *He's just a product being sold to the masses.* That was what she'd said about the Nameless Hero. And maybe she had a point.

A few hours into the photo shoot, the studio door opened, and the rest of the Alliance of the Impossible entered. It was the first time I'd seen my friends in more than a week, and just being in the same room with them boosted my mood.

Unfortunately, not everyone was as excited about our reunion. Milton stood at the edge of the group, scowling at me in a way that jolted my memory back to the argument we'd had back in my artificial bedroom. He was obviously still mad.

Once the director called a break in the shoot, I jogged

across the studio to see if I could talk him into forgiving me.

"Hey," I said. "If you're interested, I can probably hook you up with some free zit cream."

Milton didn't even chuckle. He only shrugged, grumbling something that sounded like, "Hey."

"So—um . . ." I stared down at my feet. "Sorry about what happened."

"I'm surprised you even remember that," he said. "You haven't been back since."

"Gavin won't let me. He says he doesn't want to risk paparazzi following us. So I'm stuck staying in a hotel room by myself."

"Sounds horrible." It was impossible to miss the sarcasm in his voice. "At least we get a chance to stand around watching you film your commercial, right?"

Frustration stirred inside me. I'd come over to apologize, but Milton only wanted to make things worse. When I spoke up again, I could feel anger surging behind each word.

"It's not my fault I'm more famous than you."

I wished I could get the words back as soon as I'd spoken them. Milton's expression was half surprise, half disgust, as if he couldn't believe that I'd just admitted to all the terrible things he'd been thinking about me.

"I guess what *Super Scoop* said about you is right," Milton hissed. "You *do* think you're better than the rest of us."

I stared back at him, stunned. "What're you talking about?"

Milton reached into one of the many pouches in his uniform and pulled out a rolled-up magazine.

"Here." He shoved the copy of *Super Scoop* into my hand. "Read for yourself."

Milton stomped away, leaving me alone with the magazine.

Looking down at the cover, I saw myself staring back at me. In the photo, I was striking a pose in my mask and uniform. Next to my picture was bold text that read:

THE SUPERHERO WITH NO NAME

TIFFANY COSGROVE GOES BEHIND THE MASK TO REVEAL THE SHOCKING *TRUTH* ABOUT THE NAMELESS HERO

I opened the magazine and flipped past glossy shots of superheroes walking their dogs and hanging out in cafés, until I found the article I was looking for.

The more I read, the angrier I got. Tiffany Cosgrove had made me look like some kind of spoiled celebrity superbrat—escorted everywhere in my own personal hover SUV, demanding over-the-top (and bizarre) food combinations from room service.

According to one tipster, the article stated, *the Nameless Hero refuses to spend his time in the same training facility as the rest of the Alliance of the Impossible. Instead, he demands a fancy hotel suite all to himself.*

It only got worse from there. A photo showed me next to the eight-year-old girl who'd asked for my autograph.

I was standing there with a dumbfounded look on my masked face while the girl stumbled backward. Of course, Trace had been the one to pull her out of my way. But since Trace had been invisible at the time, it looked like *I'd* just shoved the girl.

Beside the photograph was a block of bold text that read:

The Nameless Hero showing his fan how he *really* feels.

I swallowed an angry breath and went on reading. It was like witnessing one of my parents' evil schemes. No matter how upset it made me, I couldn't look away.

Cosgrove spent an entire page describing the "power struggle" between nFinity and me. *The Nameless Hero isn't satisfied with just taking the leadership role from nFinity. He's also on a mission to take nFinity's celebrity status—*

I stopped reading when I noticed out of the corner of my eye that someone was approaching. Glancing up from the page, I caught sight of something that caused my insides to squirm.

nFinity.

The magazine dropped out of my hands. A second before, I'd been reading about how much we hated each other. And now here he was. In person. It was as if he'd climbed out of the page just to punch my lights out.

I hoped he didn't take any of that as seriously as Milton had. The last thing I needed was to get into a fight with a guy whose hands doubled as flamethrowers.

I felt slightly better when nFinity flashed me an easygoing

grin. He pointed at the magazine I'd just dropped. "I do the same thing whenever I read *Super Scoop*. Except I usually drop it into the nearest trash can."

"I—I just want you to know," I spluttered, "none of that stuff is true."

"Don't worry." nFinity brushed his hair off his forehead like it was no big deal. "I've read enough lies about myself in that magazine to never trust anything they print. Actually, I just came over to say congratulations."

"Congratulations? For what?"

"The new endorsement deal. Pimple Prevention Power." nFinity patted me on the shoulder, smiling. "I'd heard they were looking for a new spokesperson for a while now."

"Really? Who was their old spokesperson?"

nFinity's smile wavered slightly. "Me."

Being the official spokesperson for advanced acne cream wasn't exactly my dream job, and I wasn't sure whether to apologize to nFinity for taking his place or offer it back to him.

I spotted Milton chatting with Sophie in the corner. I was too far away to hear what he was saying, but I had a feeling it was about me. And it was probably all bad.

I turned back to nFinity. "Can I ask you something?"

"Sure," he said. "What's up?"

"How did your friends react when you . . . uh—became famous?"

A hint of sadness passed over nFinity's features. "A nasty side effect of becoming famous is that you lose some of your best friends in the process."

186

"If that's the case, I'd rather keep my friends and not be famous."

"Unfortunately, you don't always get to choose." From the look on his face, it was obvious he was speaking from experience.

"If I could just spend a little more time with Milton at headquarters, maybe I could make things better."

"Haven't you heard? We were forced to leave. That's why Trace brought us here."

"Forced to leave?" My brain stumbled to keep up. "Why?"

nFinity lowered his voice. "Brandy went missing."

23

I felt like I'd been punched in the stomach by one of Multiplier's clones.

"Brandy's . . . missing?" I asked. "What happened?"

"Nobody knows for sure," nFinity said. "She left headquarters last night without telling anyone. Gavin's afraid she's been secretly working with Multiplier the entire time."

I shook my head. None of this made sense. "That's impossible. Brandy wouldn't do that."

I'd expected nFinity to agree with me, but he didn't seem so sure. "Gavin says she took a bunch of secret surveillance tapes from headquarters with her. He's convinced she passed them on to Multiplier so he'll be able to infiltrate headquarters. Until Gavin tracks her down, it's not safe for us there anymore."

My memory skipped back over the interactions I'd had with Brandy, wondering if there was any truth to what nFinity had said. Of all the adults involved with the Alliance of the Impossible, Brandy was the only one who actually seemed to care about me and the other kids.

Had it all been just an act?

Even if I had trouble picturing Brandy betraying us, I could at least see how she would make the perfect spy. She'd spent her entire life pretending to be someone else. Shifting from one person to another. Taking on an entirely new face and new personality each time.

Maybe she'd been doing the same with us all along.

"Okay, everyone—back to work!" The director stepped forward, waving his arms to get our attention. "If you're not a part of this shoot, then I need you out of the way. That includes you." The director turned his glare on nFinity. "Can't have you distracting our actor, now, can we?"

"I used to *be* the actor," nFinity muttered in a voice that only I could hear. He usually looked so cool, so well arranged. But for a moment, I saw a flash of bitterness on his face. For an instant it was clear: losing his place with Triple-P was a bigger disappointment than he would ever admit.

Then the look changed to something else—surprise. Following his gaze toward the side doors, I realized what had caught nFinity's attention.

A silver sphere came rolling into the studio. It was about the size of a beach ball, but from the heavy sound of it passing over the floor, I guessed it was made of metal. The ball rolled a few feet, then shifted direction just in time to avoid a bank of lights. It turned again—and again—dodging people and equipment with way too much accuracy to be a coincidence.

Someone was steering it.

The sight jolted my memory back to AwesomeWorld and the silver sphere that had fallen from the sky. This one looked the same—only a whole lot bigger. There was no question who'd been responsible the last time a mysterious silvery object had appeared out of nowhere: Phineas Vex. Was he planning to send the world another message?

I readied myself for an attack. But not everyone was so concerned.

"Okay, who brought the toy?" the director called out as the ball rolled steadily in his direction. His expression grew angrier and angrier as the sphere got closer and closer. "This isn't playtime, people! We've got work to—"

He was interrupted by a sharp *click!* The sphere snapped open like a puzzle coming apart—from one single round shape to dozens of pieces, twisting and rearranging themselves in fluid motions. The silver ball had become something else entirely.

A metal scorpion.

The thing was half my height, with a pair of ultrasharp claws, shining black eyes, and a curved tail that narrowed to a daggerlike point.

With a robotic arachnid staring him down, the director didn't look quite so angry anymore. His face went slack with fear. "Actually, I think we've got enough footage for the commercial." He gulped. "That's a wrap, folks!"

The director took off running wildly. This snapped the rest of the crew into motion. In an instant, everyone was fleeing for the exits. But they didn't get very far. More silver spheres came rolling through the doors, blocking every possible escape.

Screams filled the studio as each of the spheres popped open, their parts rearranging to become scorpions.

There were five in all. The robots edged toward us from all sides, corralling everyone as if we were sheep. Looking into the dark eyes of the nearest one made me want to retreat deeper into the crowd. But that wasn't the way things worked. At least, not while I was wearing a uniform, parading around as a famous superhero. People expected me to protect crowds, not hide in them.

"They came here for us." I raised my voice, hoping I sounded more confident than I felt. "There are five of them. One for each of us. Let's give them what they came for."

I caught a glimpse of Milton. He looked back at me grudgingly but stepped forward all the same.

The rest of the team emerged from the crowd, preparing for the fight. But when I tried to join them, Gavin gripped my arm.

"*You're* not going anywhere," he stated firmly. "I've got three weeks of publicity scheduled and an entire line of merchandise on the way. I can't risk your getting hurt."

"But they need my help," I protested.

"They'll be fine. They've prepared for this."

"You mean, while I was on the Nameless Hero celebrity tour?"

Gavin didn't say anything, but his grip on my arm tightened.

For a long moment, nobody moved. The tension crackled like static. And then Miranda took action. A scorpion lunged forward, but she was ready for it. Grabbing a nearby camera stand like it was a battle-ax, she smacked the robot sideways.

The others took this as their cue to join the fight. nFinity released a sheet of fire that sent a robot scrambling backward. Sophie sidestepped the claws of one scorpion and landed a superpowered kick in the midsection of another. Milton's rocket boots propelled him up and over an attacking robot.

But with Gavin holding me back, the Alliance of the Impossible was outnumbered. And by the looks of it, the scorpions had enough armor to withstand pretty much any attack. A blast of fire, a roundhouse to the stomach, getting whacked with camera equipment? These assaults barely fazed them.

Locked in battle with one of the robots, nFinity didn't notice another coming his way, until it was nearly too late. The scorpion's tail flicked forward with terrifying suddenness, the blade slicing through the Kevlar padding in nFinity's uniform.

Lurching backward, nFinity gripped his shoulder. Blood poured through his fingers.

The others weren't doing much better. Hovering in the

air, Milton pulled a canister out of his utility belt and dropped it onto the scorpion beneath him. The canister burst open, releasing its net a second too late. Instead of trapping the robot, it bounced off the thing's back and entangled Miranda. Sophie was backed into a corner, with two scorpions bearing down on her.

Meanwhile, I was stuck on the sidelines, feeling more like the Nameless Weenie than the Nameless Hero. I tried to tug my arm free, but Gavin held on tightly. There was no telling how much longer the others would be able to hold off the scorpions, and I wasn't about to wait around to find out.

Straining to focus, I clenched my fists. I could feel my Gyft buzzing to life inside me, a wave of energy crashing through my veins. The jolt hit Gavin all at once. He released his grip on my arm, staggering backward and gripping his hand in surprise.

I leaped forward before he had a chance to recover. Gavin's angry voice rose from the crowd behind me, but I hardly heard it. My attention was on the fight raging in front of me.

Miranda was the closest, still trying to free herself from the net wrapped around her legs. A scorpion lunged at her, its tail flicking forward like a bolt of lightning. It missed her by only a fraction of an inch. I got there before it had a chance to make a second strike.

I slammed into the scorpion's side with both hands just as another surge of spontaneous combustion flared through me.

In an instant, the scorpion exploded into a cloud of silver scrap metal. But there wasn't a lot of time to enjoy the fireworks. At one end of the studio, Sophie was struggling to hold off two of the robots. At the other end, a second pair was going after nFinity in a blur of claws and razor-sharp tails. With his injured shoulder, I doubted he'd be able to survive their attacks much longer.

Milton landed next to me. As he glanced from Sophie to nFinity, I could see him reaching the same conclusion. There was no way to help one without abandoning the other—unless we worked together.

"I'll help nFinity, and you help Sophie?" I suggested. I halfway expected Milton to ignore me out of spite. Instead, he nodded.

"Good luck," he said.

"You too."

And then we were off. On the way to nFinity's end of the studio, I passed by a table where boxes of Triple-P Advanced Acne Cream were being displayed. Without slowing down, I grabbed a jumbo-sized bottle and launched it at one of the scorpions. A pulse of energy. A flash of red. And just like that, the zit cream was transformed into a blazing missile that exploded as soon as it hit the scorpion.

I kept running. Somewhere in my peripheral vision, I caught a quick glimpse of the crew, crowded in the center of the room. Some of them had picked up cameras and were using them to film the scene that was taking place around them.

But there was no time to pose for a close-up. The remaining scorpion had nFinity backed against the wall, one hand clutched to his bloody shoulder. A swipe of the scorpion's tail grazed his leg, leaving behind a bloody gash above his knee.

I got to the robot an instant before it could move in for the kill and grabbed the thing's tail from behind. This was the point when I'd hoped the robot would blast apart and we'd all be saved. But that wasn't what happened. Using my Gyft so many times in a row had left me drained.

And the timing couldn't have been worse. Without spontaneous combustion, I was just a kid hugging the sharp end of an oversized scorpion. Not where I wanted to be.

The robot twisted to look at me. I barely had time to react before one of its claws snapped. Another moment's hesitation and the thing would've split me in two. I jumped sideways as the claw came at me again. This time it was even closer. As I sidestepped the attack, my feet tangled underneath me and I tumbled to the ground.

The scorpion leveled its gaze on me. Cold, unblinking eyes that seemed to be considering which would be the better way to kill me—cutting me in half with its claws or skewering me with its tail like a shish kebab.

I crawled backward, hands and feet scrabbling over the hard floor. The scorpion loomed over me.

Catching another glimpse of the crowd, I saw all the cameras trained on me. How many views would the Nameless Hero's death attract on YouTube?

My vision filled with a flash of silver as the robot made its move.

24

As the scorpion lunged forward, something swept over it. A net. The robot snapped backward like a dog on a leash, claws and tail swinging frantically.

The fog of panic in my mind cleared long enough for me to figure out what had happened. After freeing herself from the net, Miranda had thrown it across the robot's body. Sophie and Milton must've taken care of the other two scorpions, because they ran to join her.

Glowing in her golden uniform, Sophie grabbed one end of the net and flung it above her head, heaving the scorpion like a sack of flour. When she released her grip on the net, the robot sailed across the studio and collided with the wall in a thunderous crash of metal against brick. Robot parts clattered to the ground in a heap.

"That's the last of them." Sophie rushed to my side. "Are you all right?"

I nodded. "Just a little shaken up. But nFinity—"

"Don't worry about me," nFinity spoke up. "I'll be fine."

Sophie's eyes widened when she noticed the extent of his injuries. "What do you mean, 'fine'?" Her voice cracked with concern. "You're *bleeding*. We need to get you to a hospital."

"It's just a scratch. Really. The uniform's body armor absorbed most of the impact."

But Gavin wasn't taking any chances. "I already made a call. The doctor'll be here in twenty minutes."

While we waited, Gavin pulled me aside. I figured he was about to give me a stern lecture about how wrong it was to jolt your elders with spontaneous combustion. Or maybe he was going to yell at me for nearly getting myself killed. Instead, he smiled, patting me on the back.

"Terrific job back there, Nameless!" he exclaimed. "We got some great footage of you blowing up that robot. I'm tellin' ya, kid . . . once this hits the news, there's no telling the endorsement deals you'll be getting. Pimple Prevention Power is just the beginning!"

"Those scorpions," I said. "They were sent by Phineas Vex."

At the mention of Vex's name, Gavin's mouth twitched like he was a fish gasping for breath. Another moment passed while he composed himself. By the time he responded, it was with his usual gruff confidence.

"I seriously doubt that," he said. "This attack has Multiplier's name written all over it. With Brandy on his side, he knew we'd be here. Must've sent those things as payback for Times Square."

197

I shook my head. Something didn't add up. Since when did Multiplier send robots to do his dirty work? He had an unlimited supply of clones for that kind of thing. And I still couldn't entirely convince myself that Brandy had betrayed us. What if there was another reason for her disappearance?

But Gavin had made up his mind. "From now on, Brandy is our enemy," he said with a note of finality in his voice. "With the information she possesses, she poses a grave threat to all of us. We certainly can't go back to headquarters—no doubt she's shared the location with Multiplier. That means I've gotta find somewhere else for the rest of the group. And you."

"We can all stay together!" I blurted out.

Gavin faced me, his eyes bulging with surprise. "What?"

The idea took form in my head. "A new hotel. Five rooms. One for each of us."

"Absolutely not! There'll be no place for the group to train!"

"So we book a hotel with a fitness center."

Gavin gritted his teeth. "This isn't a good idea. You're a superstar now."

"So what? Superstars aren't supposed to have any friends?"

"Friends?" Gavin made it sound like a bad word when he said it. "Friends are a distraction. I've seen it plenty of times before. A kid with a lot of potential, and it all goes away because he'd rather hang around playing video games with *friends* than go to a photo shoot. What I'm offering you is

better than friends. I want to make you the biggest star in the world."

I stood my ground, determined not to give in. "Either you book us all in the same place or I'm through with all of this. No more TV shows, no more pimple commercials."

Gavin stared at me in silence. "Fine," he said tensely. "I'll find a hotel for all of you."

"Also, I want to train with the others. And they get to come along for more of the publicity. We're still a team. I want people to know that."

A vein throbbed on Gavin's forehead. "This is lunacy. I'll never—"

"Okay, then." I shrugged, reaching up to remove my mask.

"Wait, WAIT! Fine—it's a deal. Whatever you want."

"Good!" I had to keep myself from smiling. At least being a world-famous superhero came with a few perks.

We must've been a strange sight when we arrived at our new hotel later that day. A bunch of kids in spandex uniforms walking through the lobby. Behind us, our luggage seemed to be floating through the air. Trace was invisible, but I could tell from his groaning that he wasn't happy about carrying all our stuff.

"Isn't this *your* job?" he barked at a couple of very confused-looking bellhops standing nearby.

While Gavin checked everyone in, Milton approached

me. For a few seconds, neither of us said anything. I thought about how we'd worked together back at the studio. Did that mean we were done arguing? Or did we only get along when our lives were at stake?

"So, um . . ." Milton toed the carpet. "I heard you talked Gavin into letting everyone stay together."

I nodded. "Yeah."

"And you said you wanted to train with us?"

"Well, I wouldn't want everyone to get buff except me."

I flexed a nonexistent muscle. I couldn't be sure, but it looked to me like Milton was suppressing a laugh.

"I guess what I'm trying to say is . . ." Milton hesitated. "I'm—uh . . . sorry about . . . you know."

"Me too," I muttered. "I didn't mean for things to get so out of hand."

Milton's face broke into a smile that let me know in an instant that we were best friends again.

After we were checked in, the rest of the team met at my room. I called for room service, and while we waited, the conversation turned to Brandy.

"Over the past few days, I Sensed something about her," Miranda said. "She's been sneaking around behind Gavin's back."

"Doing what?"

Miranda shook her head. "I don't know. She's good at blocking me. So are Gavin and Trace. They're trained to keep Sensers out of their heads. But I managed to pick up a few fragments. Bits and pieces. She was hiding something. And she was worried that Gavin would find out."

"It must've been because of the security tapes," nFinity said. "She stole them. And when Gavin got suspicious, she made a run for it."

"I just don't get it," Milton said. "Why would Brandy want to work with Multiplier?"

"They were in that group together," nFinity pointed out. "X-Treme Team."

"Yeah, until Multiplier killed one of the other members and disappeared for the next fifteen years," I said.

"Maybe she's been acting as a spy for him this whole time," Sophie said.

"I don't know." Milton tugged at one of his uniform's sleeves. "She looked pretty surprised to find out he was back."

"That could've just been a part of her act," nFinity said.

Our conversation went around and around like this until we were interrupted by the arrival of room service. When I answered the door, I was still too tense to laugh as the bellhop listed the food that we'd ordered.

"Spaghetti and gummy bears. Five hamburgers dipped in chocolate sauce. French fries and pudding. A cake with potato chips sprinkled over it. And . . ." The bellhop paused, like he was trying to decide if this was all just a very weird dream. "A Belgian waffle in the shape of Abraham Lincoln's head."

"Exactly," I said.

Once the bellhop left, we all took our masks off and settled in front of the TV to eat our lunch. I was taking a bite of Abraham Lincoln's top hat when the show we'd been watching ended suddenly and was replaced by a video of a man in a purple and black uniform.

Multiplier.

His thin lips curled into a revolting grin. The way he stared out of the TV screen, it was like he was looking right at me.

"I'm sorry to interrupt your regularly scheduled programming," he said, "but I have a message for the Nameless Hero."

25

It's not every day that a supervillain hijacks national television to send me a personal message.

Multiplier glared through the TV screen. Behind him, I spotted a large object covered with a purple sheet.

"If you're watching, Nameless Hero, there are a few things I want you to know," Multiplier said. "First of all, I don't appreciate you and your friends visiting me in New York. And the way you rode one of my clones like he was your own personal subway system—not cool."

Multiplier's voice made my skin crawl. I glanced behind him again. Whatever he had under the sheet took up a lot of space. And it wasn't moving.

"Of course, I understand your motivation," Multiplier went on. "It's what you superheroes do. Heck, I used to be just like you. Flying around, fighting evil. I lived the life. Adoring fans, TV shows . . . Then it all fell apart. I was forced into hiding by the same society that had once worshipped me."

Multiplier's eyes narrowed, red under his mask.

"But eventually I had to stage my comeback. You may be familiar with some of my recent work. The Grand Canyon. Mount Rushmore. The Hollywood sign. The Statue of Liberty. All famous, beloved by people everywhere. Just as I used to be. And now, like me, they're ruined."

He turned, gesturing to whatever was under the purple sheet.

"Now I'd like to direct your attention to my most recent project. Although it isn't quite as large as the Statue of Liberty or Mount Rushmore, you'll soon discover that it stacks up quite nicely next to the other landmarks I've visited."

With a single quick motion, Multiplier grabbed the sheet and swept it away.

Behind him was a massive copper bell. But not just any bell. Along the surface ran a long crack that I recognized from my American history textbook.

Multiplier had stolen the Liberty Bell.

"My clones and I took a trip to Philadelphia," he said. "And while we were there, we picked up quite a souvenir. I'm keeping it here in a place that should be very familiar to you and your superfriends. If you want it back, you'll have to come for it. And bring the rest of the Alliance of the Impossible with you. Fail to meet my demand within two hours, and the Liberty Bell is going to have a lot more than *one* crack."

A wicked smirk passed across Multiplier's face.

"See you soon," he said.

And the screen turned to static.

Ten minutes later, we were standing in front of the hotel in our masks and uniforms, when an SUV pulled up without anyone in the driver's seat.

"Here's our ride," Sophie said, opening the door. The rest of us piled inside after her.

"So . . . um, where're we going?" Milton asked once we were flying above Manhattan.

"Multiplier said he was keeping the bell in a location that would be very familiar to all of us," Gavin said. "That can only be one of two places."

"The tanning salon or the headquarters underneath," Miranda said.

"Exactly."

Clouds drifted past the window. The tip of the Empire State Building glimmered in the sunlight below us. Soon we crossed over the river, and the tall buildings were replaced by sparse farmland and country roads. I hadn't been back to headquarters in more than a week, and now that I was finally returning, everything had changed. I'd shown up on the cover of *Super Scoop*, Brandy had betrayed us, the Liberty Bell was being held hostage by Multiplier. . . .

But at the moment, we had more immediate problems.

"We're being followed," Trace said.

When I glanced at the security monitor built into the dashboard, I saw what he meant. The screen showed a view of two men on hover cycles trailing closely behind us.

"D'you think they're working for Multiplier?" Milton asked.

"Worse," Gavin said. "They're paparazzi."

One of the guys zoomed forward until he was beside us. With the free hand that wasn't gripping the handlebars, he aimed a massive camera into the side windows of the SUV, trying to snap photos of us.

"Lose 'em," Gavin growled.

"With pleasure," Trace said.

It was a good thing we were wearing our seat belts. All of a sudden, everything rocked sideways and we plummeted toward the earth. For a few seconds there, I was sure we were going to crash. Then Trace slammed on the brakes and the seat belt strap dug into my shoulder. My stomach dropped as we rocketed upward again, performing a few loops and twists along the way. But no matter what Trace did, the paparazzi stayed close on our tail.

"It's impossible to outmaneuver them in a vehicle this size," he complained. "They're too quick."

"Then we've gotta find another way to get rid of 'em." Gavin twisted in his seat to peer angrily at the hover cycles. "We can't have the press following us back to headquarters."

"I might have an idea," I said. "It's me they're after, right?"

Gavin nodded. "A single photo of the Nameless Hero

can be worth hundreds. Thousands if you do something incredible."

"Then let's give them what they want."

When I told the others my idea, they looked at me like I was crazy. But nobody else was coming up with any other solutions, and we were running short on time. If we didn't get back to headquarters soon, Multiplier was going to turn the Liberty Bell into scrap metal.

Milton and I climbed into the back of the SUV. The first part of my plan was easy enough—switch uniforms. Once we were done, Milton pulled my mask over his head and turned to me. "How do I look?"

"Like me," I admitted. "Only taller."

The only thing we didn't exchange was our boots.

"Won't anyone wonder why the Nameless Hero suddenly has rocket-shoes?" he asked.

"They'll just assume I upgraded," I said.

Milton nodded. And just like that, the back of the SUV popped open. Waves of wind rushed through the vehicle. I gripped the side, watching the two photographers weave through the sky behind us on their hover cycles.

As Milton inched closer to the opening, he glanced back at me. I could see excitement mixed with fear in his eyes.

"It's not too late to back out!" I yelled over the sound of the wind. "We can figure out some other way!"

He shook his head. "I can do it!"

Milton hesitated a second longer. Then he jumped.

The paparazzi wavered for a second in the air as they watched the Nameless Hero fall to the earth. Then they directed their hover cycles after him.

After Milton dropped a few hundred feet, his jet-boots kicked in. He shot across the sky, swerving and twisting as the two cycles whizzed behind him.

"They bought it!" Sophie grinned at me. "They think Milton is you!"

I watched through the window, amazed that the plan was actually working. The official explanation for why Milton was the one jumping out of the SUV instead of me was that he knew how to operate the jet-propulsion boots. But it didn't hurt that he also did such a great job of acting like the Nameless Hero. Flying through the sky, trailed everywhere by photographers . . . Milton actually seemed to be enjoying himself. He performed a few backflips, then paused to grin and flex his muscles for the cameras. I had to admit, he was a much better celebrity superhero than I'd ever been.

After a few more poses for the paparazzi, the hover cycles moved in for a close-up. That was when Milton reached into his utility belt and grabbed hold of a gray canister. It looked exactly like what he'd used earlier on the scorpions.

But this one didn't release a net. It had a completely different function. . . .

"Everyone cover your eyes!" I screamed as Milton tossed the canister at the photographers.

Even with my hands clamped over my eyes, I could tell what happened next. A burst of light filled the sky, like an explosion of lightning, temporarily blinding anyone who looked at it.

By the time I opened my eyes again, Milton was climbing back into the SUV and the paparazzi were wobbling back down to earth. They'd get their vision back in time to safely land their hover cycles. But by then, we'd be long gone.

When we landed in the parking lot of Tantastic an hour later, Milton and I had changed back into our own uniforms. I looked out the window, searching for any sign of Multiplier, but all I saw was a normal shopping center on a normal afternoon.

"This'll get you through the front door," Gavin said, handing me a key. "We'll be right here in the SUV. You've all got walkie-talkies in your utility belts. Use them to contact us if anything goes wrong."

I stepped out of the SUV, my heart pounding. I'd spent enough time around supervillains to know that Multiplier hadn't called us here to chat about our summer plans. He had something much worse in mind. And we were about to find out what it was.

Crossing the parking lot drew some odd looks. People were definitely surprised to see their afternoon shopping interrupted by five underage superheroes rushing toward a tanning salon.

"Are you sure we should be doing this?" I asked.

"What other choice do we have?" nFinity said. "We can't let him ransack any more landmarks. Besides, we beat him once before. We can beat him again."

I still wasn't certain. The last time had felt like a fluke. And now we didn't know *what* was waiting for us inside.

The sign hanging from the front door of Tantastic read CLOSED. I peered through the window. The place was empty. Everything looked the same as it had the last time I'd been there—with one huge difference.

The Liberty Bell was sitting in the corner.

It looked even bigger up close. Propped up on a metal stand, the bell was more than twice my height and probably weighed as much as my parents' Volvo.

"You don't think Multiplier just . . . left it here?" Milton asked.

"Only one way to find out." I slid the key into the lock and pushed open the front door a half inch. When nothing horrible happened, I pushed it the rest of the way and cautiously stepped inside. The others followed.

The five of us huddled at the front of the store next to a rack of sunscreen. Somehow it made me *more* nervous that we hadn't been attacked yet. I tried to keep calm. Maybe there was a reasonable explanation for why the Liberty Bell was just sitting there, unguarded. Maybe Multiplier felt guilty and had turned himself in to the local authorities. But as much as I tried to repeat this fantasy to myself, I knew there had to be another reason—something much worse.

"This seems too easy," Sophie said.

"It *is* too easy." Miranda's voice shook. "Everyone be careful."

"Careful of *what*?" Milton said. "I bet Multiplier just got scared when he saw us coming and made a run for it. I'm gonna take a closer look—"

"Milton, NO!" Miranda reached out to grab Milton, but it was already too late. He took a step forward. That was when we all heard it—

BEEP!

It was barely more than an electronic chirp, but the noise echoed loudly in my head. There must've been a laser sensor in the room. And Milton had just stepped across it.

Milton froze. "What just happened?"

"You set off a trap." Miranda pointed to the Liberty Bell. Purple gas had begun pouring out of the bottom of it, like a poisonous fog spreading across the room.

The five of us turned at once to escape, but that was as far as we got. A metal grate was lowering in front of the entryway. My heart seized with fear as I watched the grate fall, blocking any view into the salon—and any way out.

Next to the exit was the rack of suntan lotion we'd passed by on the way into the salon. But at the time, I'd failed to notice the bottle on the middle rack with a label that read:

Multiplier's Own SleepyTime Gas
Extra-Effective Superhero Formula
Have a nice nap!

A stream of purple gas spewed out of the top of the bottle. I held my breath and rushed straight into the fog, focusing my Gyft in the hopes of blasting our way out. By now, the air was so thick with purple gas, it was impossible to see where I was going. I staggered one more step toward the door, suddenly dizzy. And that's the last thing I remember.

26

I don't know how long I was out. A few minutes? A few hours? All I know is that I woke up with a crushing headache and a couple of Multipliers looking down at me from on top of the Liberty Bell.

Not the nicest thing to see when you wake up.

I was still inside the tanning salon. It was impossible to tell the time of day or night. The metal grate covered the front of the salon. I glanced around for the others, and my heart sank. They were gone.

"Look who's awake!" said one of the Multipliers.

"It's everyone's favorite tween superhero," said the other. This made them both laugh like it was the funniest thing they'd ever heard.

I tried to climb to my feet, but something held me in place. Twisting around, I saw that my wrists had been chained to a pipe behind me.

"In case you're thinking about busting out of those chains, don't bother," one of the villains said. "Your spontaneous compunction won't work."

"It's spontaneous *combustion*," I corrected. "And what're you talking about?"

"The gas that knocked you out also neutralizes superpowers. So unless you've got a pair of bolt cutters hidden under those sparkly spandex sleeves of yours, it looks like you're stuck here with us."

This set the supervillains laughing again. The one on the right cackled so hard that he kicked the Liberty Bell, sending a deafening noise reverberating through the room. Maybe it had something to do with the crack in the side of the bell, but the sound wasn't really a ring. More like a metallic thud. A very LOUD metallic thud.

"Where're my friends?" I asked once my ears stopped buzzing.

"Your superbuddies?" said the one on the left, still chuckling. "They're locked away with Gavin and Trace downstairs."

"*Waaaaay* downstairs," said the other.

"Headquarters?" I asked.

The Multipliers nodded. "One is keepin' an eye on 'em."

"One?"

"The original. You know, Multiplier One-Point-Oh."

"You're his clones?"

"*I'm* his clone," said the Multiplier on the left, his voice thick with pride. He pointed at the villain beside him. "And he's *my* clone."

214

The clone's clone frowned a little at this comment. And he looked even more disgruntled when Multiplier Number Two nudged him with an elbow and ordered him to double-check the metal grate. Grumbling, he hopped down from his perch on top of the Liberty Bell and did as he was told.

The chain rattled behind me, digging into my wrists. The situation was looking more and more hopeless. My friends were being held captive half a mile beneath the Earth's surface. The only other people who knew I was here were Gavin and Trace, but they were locked away too. My house was just a few minutes' drive from here, but my parents still thought I was off at Gyfted kids' summer camp. If only there were some way I could signal them. But how was I supposed to do *that* when I was powerless and chained against the wall?

Then I realized it. . . . I didn't have to signal them. Not if one of the clones did it for me.

"Hey, Number Three," I said. "I was just wondering. . . . How's it feel?"

Multiplier Number Three looked up from the doorway, where he was checking the grate. "How's *what* feel?"

"Being the clone of a clone. Always getting bossed around by the clone above you. Must get frustrating."

Multiplier Number Three scratched his head. "Now that you mention it, it *does* get kind of old."

"You know, if you had your own clone, he could do that *for* you."

"He's messing with your head," grunted Number Two. "Don't listen to him."

"See, there he goes again," I said to Number Three. "Bossing you around, like always."

"Y'know something? You're right!" Multiplier Number Three abandoned his work and turned to glare at Number Two. "I'm sick of being told what to do. I'll make a clone of my own. Then *he'll* do whatever *I* want!"

"Don't you dare!" Multiplier Number Two screamed, but it didn't do any good. A loud *POP* sounded and a third Multiplier appeared.

"Well, hello there!" The newest clone glanced around at the inside of the tanning salon like he was impressed, his eyes passing over the Liberty Bell in the corner, the super-hero chained to the wall.

"Looks like a party's goin' on in here!" he said. "Thanks for invitin' me!"

"You're welcome," said Number Three. "Now check on that security grate. We don't want anyone getting inside."

Multiplier Number Four's voice took on a whiny tone. "Aawww! I just got here!" He stomped his foot like a kid who doesn't want to clean his room. "Why do I have to do everything?"

"Because I said so!" Number Three sounded excited to be the one giving the orders, not receiving them. "Now get to it!"

"Tell you what," countered Number Four. "I'll just make another clone. Then at least I'll have someone to help me."

"No! That's not the way it's supposed to work!"

Multiplier Number Two hopped down from his perch

atop the Liberty Bell. Crossing his arms smugly, he said, "Not so funny now, is it?"

Over the sounds of Number Three's protests, another *POP* jolted through the tanning salon. And—just like that—there were four Multipliers. Turned out the newest clone was even *less* willing to do the job than the others, and before anyone could stop him, he created *another* clone . . . and that one created a clone too . . . and—

POP! POP! POP!

Before long, the tanning salon was jammed with identical purple and black supervillains. There were too many to count. And still, none of them stepped forward to fix the security grate. Instead, Multipliers stood around chatting with each other by the tanning booth. Others were at the counter, attempting to break into the cash register. A few more were trying on sunglasses near the door.

It was pretty easy to pick out which clones had been created most recently. They were clumsier—or just plain dumber—than the rest of the group. One of them stumbled across the tanning salon with a cross-eyed expression on his face, asking where he could find the nearest taco stand. Another was sitting cross-legged on the floor, guzzling a bottle of sunscreen.

It was just like Brandy had said. Each new copy was a little bit duller than the last. And easier to control. Or at least, I hoped so.

I caught the eye of the clone who'd been drinking the sunscreen. "Hey, you know what's *really* fun?"

The clone set down the bottle. "Whuh?"

I glanced across the room. All the other clones were too preoccupied to notice our conversation. My eyes landed on the Liberty Bell. "See that bell over there?"

The clone nodded. "Big bell."

"I wonder what it would sound like to ring the big bell. Pretty cool, I bet."

His dull gaze intensified. The clone climbed to his feet and stumbled across the salon, muttering, "Wanna ring the big bell."

I was almost too nervous to watch. Any second, I was sure one of the others would stop him. But the clone party was really heating up now, and nobody paid any attention to what one of their dimmest copies was up to.

The clone hesitated in front of the Liberty Bell, wiping a spot of sunscreen off his chin. Then he reached forward and gave the bell a hard push.

CLAAAANG!

The sound echoed in my brain like a bomb had gone off. All clone conversation came to an instant stop. Everyone turned to look at the sunscreen-loving clone who'd made all the noise. Excited by all the attention, he gave the bell another push.

"STOP THAT!" Multiplier Number Two screamed over the noise. "STEP AWAY FROM THE NATIONAL LANDMARK!"

But his scolding went ignored. And while some of the Multipliers winced and covered their ears, others clapped enthusiastically, grinning at the bell like it was a carnival attraction.

"My turn! My turn!" said one as the ringing died down.

"Lemme take a crack at it!" said another.

"Me too!" squealed a third. "And after this, we should see if there are any taco stands nearby!"

Before long, a crowd of clones was kicking and pushing the Liberty Bell from all sides. They laughed as its off-pitch clanging echoed through the salon. It was like a hammer beating against my eardrums. But at least that meant it was loud. Maybe even loud enough to be heard at my parents' house.

Trying to cover his ear with one hand, Multiplier Number Two reached into his utility belt with the other and whipped a plasma pistol from its holster. "STOP IT! NOW!"

When his command went ignored, he pulled the trigger, and a beam of red light shot out of the end, blasting a clone into a pile of dust. I winced at the sight, but reminded myself that the clones weren't real people. They were copies.

"Next one of you that *touches* the bell gets a taste of plasma," Multiplier Number Two roared. "Got it? I'm the Number Two. And since Number One's down in the headquarters, that means I'm in charge around here. So from now on, you'll do what I say, or else—"

ZAAAP!

Multiplier Number Two disintegrated before my eyes.

The clone nearest to him lowered his plasma pistol. "Looks like you ain't in charge anymore," he said.

"Hey, you can't just go around shootin' clones!" cried one of the Multipliers.

"Oh, yeah? Watch me!"

A red beam shot across the tanning salon, and another clone disappeared. After that, the scene inside the tanning salon turned into all-out war. Purple and black super-villains scrambled for their weapons, blasting each other into oblivion.

Plasma beams burst through the air in every direction. One stray shot connected with the tanning bed, turning our only ride down to headquarters into a pile of charred dust. I ducked as a rack of bronzing cream dematerialized nearby. Huddling closer to the wall, I did my best to avoid having the same thing happen to me.

The fighting finally came to an end when there was only a single clone left standing. By now, the salon was a complete wreck. The racks and shelves that hadn't been dematerialized were lying on their sides; tanning accessories spilled out across the floor. Somehow the Liberty Bell had made it through everything in one piece—even if it was one *cracked* piece.

The single remaining clone clutched his plasma pistol, slowly scanning the room. When his eyes landed on me, a dark grin twisted across his thin face.

"Well, well," he said. "Lookie what we have here."

The clone took a step toward me. A pair of sunglasses cracked beneath his foot with a sudden *cruuunch*.

"Looks like me and you are all alone, Nameless *Zero*," he said. "Just think how happy Number One will be when he finds out that I killed my very own superhero."

My heart pounded furiously. The chain rattled behind me.

"Number One wants me alive," I said. "That's why he made sure to keep me here."

The clone paused, giving this some thought. But then the evil grin returned. He aimed his plasma pistol at my chest.

"Yeah, well, Number One ain't here," he said. "Neither are Two, Three, and Four. So I guess that puts *me* in charge."

The clone took another step in my direction. Reaching out with his free hand, he pulled off my mask. When he saw my face, his lip curled into an awful smirk. I shivered as his finger tightened around the trigger.

Clenching my eyes shut, I held my breath. A burst of noise rang in my ears.

For a second I was sure it was all over. But it wasn't the blast of a plasma pistol. It was the sound of the metal grate breaking apart. In a flash of realization, it occurred to me that the clones never had gotten around to securing it. When I opened my eyes, I saw a wall of metal crashing to the floor and a dumpy robot with paddles for feet lurching into the salon. The clone whirled around, but before he could get off a shot, Elliot rammed into him, and knocked the clone to the floor.

My robot butler wobbled to look at me with his big glowing eyes.

"You ringed, sir?"

27

I'd seen Elliot respond to the ringing of a tiny bell at home. And now I knew that the call worked on a much bigger scale.

"You saved me, Elliot!" He might not have been all that great at cooking or cleaning (or much of anything else), but Elliot had really come through when I needed him most.

"Howzz camp?" he asked.

"Actually, I never really went to camp," I admitted.

"Apparently not," came another voice that I recognized instantly.

"Mom!" I screamed.

She was standing in the shattered doorway, dressed in full supervillain mode. As soon as I called her name, my mom's face broke into a tearful smile. She rushed across the tanning salon, kicking aside an upturned rack of suntan lotion before grasping me in a huge hug.

With her hands on my shoulders, Mom leaned back to give me a closer look. Her face was slick with tears of shock and relief. Her questions came pouring out so quickly that I could barely understand her.

"Why are you chained up inside a tanning salon?" she asked. "What's with the uniform? Was Multiplier just pointing a *plasma pistol* at you?"

"Umm . . . ," I said. But that was as far as I got. Just then, I saw my dad. He must've gotten dressed in a hurry. He'd missed a button on his dark gray jumpsuit, and his silver goggles were a little crooked.

"Joshua!" he called, crossing the room to hug me.

In breathless tones, they explained what had happened. Fifteen minutes before, they'd both been asleep in their bed when they'd been awakened by a sudden crash. Dad had raced downstairs just in time to see Elliot breaking down the front door of our house to follow the sound of a ringing bell in the distance. Dressed in their pajamas, Mom and Dad had jumped into the car to follow him. Luckily, they kept a spare set of Dread Duo uniforms in a secret compartment in the backseat.

"But how'd you get here?" Dad picked my mask up off the ground. He glanced from the mask to my uniform, confusion spreading across his features. "And why are you dressed like the Nameless Hero?"

I sighed. "Because I *am* the Nameless Hero."

My parents stood in expectant silence, as if they were waiting for me to say that this was all a cruel practical joke. When that didn't happen, Dad said, "But . . . how?"

I started from the beginning, describing the mysterious notes I'd received and the substitute librarian who had attacked my friends and me, how Gavin had recruited us, and how I'd accidentally become a celebrity overnight.

As I spoke, I watched their faces carefully to see if they were upset to learn that their only son was also a famous superhero—exactly the kind of person they'd spent half their lives fighting. But they both looked much too grateful that I was alive to be angry that I'd gone against the family business.

"The important thing is that you're okay!" Mom said. Her eyes moved to my outfit. "And at least they did nice work on your uniform. This looks like the handiwork of the Smicks." She pinched the spandex between her fingers.

"You've heard of the Smicks?" I asked, surprised.

"Of course we have. They got their start designing uniforms for supervillains. Including us. But then they started booking projects for superheroes, and suddenly they were *too important* to work with villains anymore. Typical." Mom exhaled an angry breath, then cast another glance at my uniform. "They may be pompous three-headed jerks, but there's no mistaking their talent."

"Now let's get you out of these chains," Dad said.

He reached into his utility belt and removed a slim plastic container from one of its many pouches.

"This oughta do the trick!" With an excited grin, Dad leaned over my shoulder and began unscrewing the container. "Metal-eating ants! One of my own inventions!"

"Wait!" My chains clattered. "I don't want a bunch of ants crawling over me."

"It's okay, Joshua. They're not real. They're miniature robotic insects with ultrasharp teeth."

"You're not making me feel better."

"Not to worry, son." Dad shook the container, gazing at it with the kind of pride he always got whenever it came to his own inventions. "They won't eat human flesh. The only material they're interested in is metal. They'll chew through those chains in no time—"

"Or we could just use this," Mom interrupted. She was holding up a key. "I found it on the counter."

A look of disappointment crossed Dad's face. "Fine. If you want to do it the *easy* way."

Once she'd unlocked the chain, Mom clasped it around the clone, who was still lying on the floor where he'd been knocked out by Elliot. As the lock clicked into place, the clone lurched forward, moaning to himself.

"I just had the worst dream that I got attacked by a trash can with feet," he mumbled.

"That wasn't a dream," Mom said.

"And it wasn't a trash can either," Dad piped up defensively. "You got attacked by a very sophisticated, state-of-the-art robot butler."

Behind him, Elliot was approaching the Liberty Bell with a roll of duct tape. "I fix the craaaaaack!" he said in his slurring electronic tone.

"Not now, Elliot!" Dad ordered.

The clone rattled his chains. He flinched when he noticed

that my mom was now holding his plasma pistol. Then his expression changed—from fear to recognition.

"Hey, you're the Botanist!" His voice was a mixture of fear and admiration. His eyes grew even wider when he saw my dad. "And you're Dr. Dread!"

"Yeah, and we're also the parents of the kid you were about to dematerialize," Mom said.

The clone went pale under his mask. "I—I wasn't gonna do anything to him, I swear. I was just . . . showin' him how the plasma pistol works."

"What a coincidence! *I* was about to show him how it works too. By blasting you into a pile of dust." Mom flashed her most supervillainous scowl.

The clone shivered with fear. "Please—I don't want to disintegrate!" he sobbed.

I'd seen my mom in action enough to know how intimidating she could be. And I also knew how to play along.

"Maybe we'll let you live," I said to the clone. "*If* you tell us what we want to know."

He nodded eagerly. "I'll tell you anything. Just don't shoot."

"Where's Number One? Is he still down in headquarters with the others?"

"Not exactly."

"What d'you mean? Where is he, then?"

A strange grin took form on the clone's face. "Actually, he's right behind you."

Mom and I spun around at the same time. Standing in the front doorway was Multiplier. Holding a plasma pistol to my dad's head.

28

Multiplier's grip on Dad tightened, his finger quivering over the trigger.

"Any sudden moves and I shoot," he said.

"Let my dad go," I said. "It's me you want. Not him."

Multiplier peered at me from across the salon. There was something in his eyes, something that was both familiar and unfamiliar at the same time.

What happened next was doubly surprising. First, Multiplier released my dad. And second, his features began to transform, until I was looking into a face that I hadn't seen in days.

"Brandy!" I gasped.

She smiled faintly. "Sorry to scare you like that, Joshua. I couldn't risk anyone realizing it was me, so I went undercover as Multiplier. Then I saw the Dread Duo lurking around the store. I had no idea you were related."

"Wait a minute . . ." Dad's head swiveled from Brandy to me. "You two *know* each other?"

I nodded. "She was part of the group that recruited me. But then she—"

Disappeared. Went missing. Suddenly, all of Gavin's warnings about Brandy went flickering through my mind. She'd betrayed us. Revealed the secret location of our facility to Multiplier. She was our enemy now.

"I'm on your side," she assured me. "It's Gavin you need to worry about."

"Gavin?"

"He's been lying to you the entire time. He lied to all of us. He's dangerous."

My head was swimming with uncertainty. Gavin was a lot of things—greedy, short-tempered, hairy. But dangerous?

I didn't know what to think anymore. I'd just started believing that Brandy was the enemy. Now I had to wrap my mind around the idea that *Gavin* was actually the one who'd been betraying us?

I stared at Brandy warily from across the salon. "How do I know you're telling the truth?"

"Because I have proof," Brandy said. "I'd begun suspecting that Gavin was lying. And so when he was away in New York, I searched his office. And what I discovered was too awful to believe."

Miranda was right. Brandy *had been* sneaking around behind Gavin's back. But what did it all mean?

"I'm not the one who's been secretly collaborating with

Multiplier. Gavin is. But it's worse than that. They're both working for Phineas Vex."

At the mention of Vex's name, a shiver went through my parents. "Do you know where Vex is?" Dad asked.

Brandy nodded. "He's closer than you think."

I glanced around, as if Vex might jump out from behind a rack of self-tanning lotion. "What're you talking about?"

"He's in the headquarters," Brandy said, her eyes never leaving mine. "He's been there since the beginning. He's—he's extremely weak. Unable to move. Hooked up to all kinds of machines."

Brandy's words hit me like a wave. All the time my friends and I had spent in headquarters, Vex had been there too. And somehow I knew—even without Brandy needing to tell me—where he'd been all along.

The room with the black door.

My memory drifted back to the inside of the black room. The wires and instrument panels. The pounding rhythm that had sounded so much like a heartbeat. That was because it *had* been a heartbeat.

A queasy feeling came over me. Miranda and I had been in the same room as Vex and we hadn't even known it.

"Once I found out what was going on, I knew I needed more proof," Brandy said. "So last night I took the surveillance tapes with me and left headquarters."

"Gavin said you gave the tapes to Multiplier. That's why everyone was forced to leave."

Brandy laughed darkly. "I'm sure Gavin *was* afraid of my sharing those tapes. But not with Multiplier. He didn't want me showing them to the media. Or the police. And that was exactly what I was going to do. But when I learned what Vex and Gavin had planned for tonight, I knew I needed to come here. Before it was too late."

"What're they planning?" Dad asked. "You mean this whole thing goes beyond stealing the Liberty Bell and taking our son hostage?"

Brandy nodded. "Way beyond." She reached into her handbag and removed a USB storage drive. "There's something you need to see."

With Elliot watching over the chained-up clone, Brandy led us behind the counter, where she inserted the drive into the side of the cash register. As soon as she did, a video monitor rose from the counter.

"There are several hours of surveillance video stored on this drive," she explained.

I thought about all those tiny cameras, watching over everything in headquarters. I'd grown so used to seeing them—after a while I'd practically stopped noticing them at all. Although I'm sure they never stopped noticing *me*.

Brandy hit a few other buttons on the cash register. The screen flickered with black-and-white surveillance video of a place that I instantly recognized. The black room. Shadows fell across everything. Wires and tubes stretched like vines toward some kind of machine.

Except this time, there was someone standing in front of the machine. Even in the darkness, I recognized the short, bald man instantly.

Gavin.

"This was recorded the day after you fought with Multiplier in Times Square," Brandy said, hitting a button on the cash register.

The video began to play. On the screen, I watched as Gavin took a step toward the machinery.

"I apologize for keeping you waiting, sir." He spoke in a quavering voice. "The past days have been extremely busy. But I have good news. The confrontation with Multiplier was a success. Everything went as planned. Well . . . *nearly* everything—"

"What do you mean?" The voice came from the shadows inside the machinery. I knew at once who it belonged to: Phineas Vex. The awful tone was like something out of my worst nightmares. "Tell me what happened," Vex commanded.

"You see, sir, ever since the fight in Times Square, Joshua Dread has become—well . . ."

"He's become *what*?"

Gavin trembled. "Famous."

"What difference does that make?"

"The thing is . . . I w-worry about the effect of his new celebrity status. If he disappears, every newspaper, website, and magazine on earth will want to know what happened. Perhaps we should wait before proceeding with our plan—"

"THERE WILL BE NO CHANGES TO THE PLAN!" Vex's voice seemed to shake the video monitor we were watching. "Our agreement was clear. I give you the money for your new superhero team. And in exchange, you bring me Joshua Dread."

My stomach curled into a sickening knot. Everything Gavin had told me was a lie. He didn't care about training me to use my Gyft or about making me into a superhero. He'd been planning to hand me over to Vex the entire time.

I could see my parents out of the corner of my eye. In the pale, flickering light of the monitor, their faces looked shocked and furious, as if they wanted to reach through the screen and strangle Vex.

But for now, all we could do was watch. In the darkness, Vex's voice hissed, "And remember, the boy must be brought to me alive. He's no good to me dead."

I stared at the screen, my mind numb with shock. What did Vex want with me? And if he hated me so much, why did he insist on keeping me alive?

"I assure you—I intend to follow through on our plan," Gavin whimpered. "I merely thought—now that the boy has become a celebrity—"

"You could exploit his fame?" Vex suggested.

Gavin shook his head. "Of course not! B-but it might be wise to wait until the media isn't following him quite so closely anymore. To make sure nobody else finds out what really happened."

"Nonsense! I have waited long enough already. We must act at the preordained time. That is when I take my new form."

I squeezed the edge of the counter more tightly. *New*

form? What was he talking about? I leaned forward but could see nothing of Vex. Only wires and machinery, surrounded by shadows.

"Once you've taken this . . . this new form"—Gavin shivered—"and I've brought you Joshua Dread, then my end of the deal is complete? Right? The rest of the team will remain unharmed? And the headquarters will be mine—for good?"

"That is correct. You will have your little team of superheroes." Vex spat out the last word like it left a foul taste in his mouth. "And your state-of-the-art training facility. I'll have no need for it—*or you*—once I get what I want."

I was so glued to the video that I hardly noticed Elliot bumbling around, trying to straighten up the mess inside the salon. As usual, his attempts to clean only made things worse. He stepped on a bottle of sunscreen, spewing lotion across the floor. Bending down to clean *that* up, he knocked a small plastic container off the counter.

None of us realized what was inside the container until it hit the ground. The cap popped off and a horde of tiny robotic bugs came crawling out. All of a sudden, my dad screamed—

"THE METAL-EATING ANTS—THEY'RE ESCAPING!"

This was about the time when the situation went from really bad to code-red catastrophic.

29

It took my brain a split second to catch up with the chaos breaking loose all around me. The container of metal-eating ants. Dad had originally gotten it out to free me from the chain. Once it was no longer necessary, he probably should've returned it to his utility belt. Instead, he'd absentmindedly placed the container on the counter and forgotten about it. At least until the moment when Elliot had knocked it to the ground, sending a flurry of robotic ants in every direction.

Elliot lurched across the floor chasing after the ants, while the ants seemed even more interested in chasing after *him*. His eyes glowed bright with a look of genuine fear when he realized what was going on.

"BAD ANTS TRYYYYING TO EAT MEEEEE!" he wailed.

Dad's face twisted with an expression of intense pain. His inventions were attacking each other.

"Elliot, you have to get out of here!" Dad stumbled across the salon, knocking the metal-eating ants away from his robot butler. He and Elliott staggered through the broken doorway and into the parking lot. Elliot hopped up and down while Dad circled him frantically, trying to shake the ants off.

It was a good thing there weren't any people in the parking lot this late at night. They might have wondered why a supervillain and a trash can with legs appeared to be dancing outside a tanning salon.

Meanwhile, Brandy and my mom were desperately trying to stop the ants from getting to the Liberty Bell, scooping the little robotic insects back into the plastic container before they could turn a national landmark into an all-you-can-eat metal buffet.

That was when I remembered the clone in the corner. I rushed across the salon, but the metal-eating ants had beaten me there. They'd already chewed through his chains, and now the clone was on his feet, an awful leer plastered across his face.

He bolted past me, pausing at the counter long enough to hit a red button at the top of the cash register. An alarm began ringing at earsplitting volume.

"So long, suckers!" the clone screamed above the alarm, rushing out the front door. Dad was too busy clearing away the last of the ants to notice the clone that raced past him and disappeared into the night.

Brandy hurried over to the counter and punched several keys on the cash register, shutting off the alarm.

"This is bad," Brandy said. "This is *very* bad. If Multiplier thinks something's gone wrong, there's no telling what he'll do. We need to get down to headquarters—*now*."

"How're we gonna do that?" I glanced toward the pile of charred dust where the tanning bed used to be. "Our ride's not looking so good."

Brandy thought for a moment. "There *is* another way."

Mom and I followed Brandy into the parking lot, where Dad was staring down sadly at the squished robotic insects around his feet.

"Took me six months to build those metal-eating ants," he said in a regretful voice. "And six minutes to destroy them."

Elliot didn't sound nearly as upset. "Baaad ants!" he droned, stepping on a few of them to make sure they'd been completely destroyed.

"Here." Mom handed the plastic container to Dad. "At least we managed to retrieve a few."

Around us, streetlights glowed in the darkness. My pulse quickened as I thought of the others down in headquarters, still unaware that Gavin was working with Vex. We had to help them before it was too late.

If it wasn't too late already.

Brandy led us across the parking lot, past other stores

in the shopping center. "Most of these are just ordinary shops," she explained. "But Tantastic wasn't the *only* portal to headquarters. Vex needed a secret way to transport cargo that wouldn't fit in the tanning bed. Something much bigger. So he used this place."

Brandy came to a stop at a glass storefront. I looked at the logo on the door.

Smoothie Sensations

"The supersecret cargo transport is . . . a smoothie shop?"

"Exactly." Brandy inserted a key and pushed open the front door. The rest of us followed her inside.

"So where's the elevator?" I asked, looking around.

"You're standing in it." Brandy moved behind the counter, past gleaming refrigerators and sinks, until she reached a row of blenders. Stuck to one of these blenders was a sign that read, OUT OF ORDER. Brandy removed the sign and pressed several of the buttons that lined the base of the blender—one after the other—as if punching in a security code.

CHOP . . . CRUSH ICE . . . LIQUEFY . . . CHOP . . . DELUXE

All at once, everything shifted into motion. I watched with surprise as the sidewalk rose higher and higher in the window. But the sidewalk *wasn't* rising. *We* were sinking. Before long, the smoothie shop had submerged beneath the earth completely.

"Quite a cargo elevator you have here," Dad said, sounding impressed.

Normally, I would've been pretty amazed too. Heck, I

probably would've made myself a smoothie for the ride. But right then, I was too worried about the others.

Along the way, we discussed what to do once we reached headquarters.

"Nobody else knows the truth about Gavin," Brandy said. "Not even Trace. Multiplier has them all locked in a holding cell. That way, Gavin can claim he's innocent."

"But if Multiplier heard the alarm, he'll be expecting intruders," Mom pointed out.

"And if we try to take him by surprise, there's a risk that he'll harm the other children," Dad said.

"Don't forget, everyone trusts Gavin. And they think you're a traitor," I said to Brandy.

The conversation dropped away into silence. I listened to the groaning of cables carrying us deeper into the ground.

It wasn't until we'd nearly reached headquarters that Brandy's eyes lit up and the faint trace of a smile appeared on her lips. "I think I might know a way. . . ."

30

When the smoothie shop finally came to a halt, Brandy led us hurriedly through headquarters. Except she didn't look like Brandy anymore. She'd Shifted along the way, changing into someone who was shorter, balder, and fatter.

She looked exactly like Gavin.

"Are you sure this is going to work?" I asked.

"Not entirely," Brandy said in Gavin's gravelly voice. "But it's the best chance we've got."

At a pair of double doors, she paused, taking a deep breath and mumbling something about "getting into character." Then she grabbed hold of my mom and shoved a plasma gun into her side with one hairy-knuckled hand.

"Sorry about that," she said. "Now, remember, you're my hostages. Got it?"

Dad and I held our hands above our heads, trying to

look scared. Elliot paddled from side to side, letting out an electronic moan.

"Good enough." Brandy pushed a button on the wall, and the doors slid open.

Multiplier spun around. His face filled with shock at the sight of Gavin. And I could understand why. Inside the holding cell was another Gavin, who looked identical to the one Brandy was impersonating. A surge of relief shot through me when I saw who was with him in the holding cell: Sophie, Milton, Miranda, nFinity, and Trace. Their weapons and utility belts had been taken, but at least they looked okay.

Multiplier fumbled for his plasma pistol and aimed it at us.

"Put that thing down," Brandy snapped, doing a perfect impression of Gavin. "I'm on your side. Caught these two supervillains in the tanning salon, along with their robot. They dematerialized your clones before I captured the Botanist here."

Brandy jabbed my mom with the plasma gun.

"Don't hurt her—please!" Dad wasn't the best actor, but his fear sounded real enough.

"It was too dangerous to leave them in the salon," Brandy said. "So I triggered the alarm and brought them here. We'll wait and see what the boss wants to do when he arrives."

Multiplier stared at us for a moment longer before he finally found his voice. "Y-you can't possibly be here," he stuttered. "You're over there."

He pointed across the room at the holding cell. From behind the clear wall, Gavin looked pretty surprised to see himself standing in the doorway. Then recognition passed over his features.

"Brandy!" His voice was muffled behind the wall of the cell, but his anger was clear enough. "She must've come back and Shifted to look like me."

"Don't listen to that imposter!" Brandy-Gavin said. "She tied me up, faked her disappearance, and has been impersonating me ever since."

"Nonsense!" The real Gavin pounded against the clear wall of the holding cell.

"She was sick of taking orders. She wanted to lead the group. So she took my place."

Multiplier glanced back and forth from one Gavin to the other, looking more frazzled by the second.

"I'll prove that I'm the real Gavin," Brandy-Gavin said next to me. "Only I know about how we've been working together with Phineas Vex the whole time. Stealing the Liberty Bell was really just a ploy to capture the Nameless Hero."

"She's lying!" Gavin shouted. "*I'm* the one who arranged everything with Phineas Vex! I'm the real G—"

Gavin slapped a hand over his mouth before he could blurt out anything else. But he'd said enough already. It no longer mattered which one was real—they'd both just admitted that they'd been lying to us the whole time.

With Multiplier distracted, Dad stepped forward and karate-chopped the plasma gun out of his hand. Mom grabbed hold of Multiplier's arm and twisted it until he fell to his knees.

"Baaaad guy fell dowwwwwn!" Elliot hopped from side to side, his eyes glowing excitedly.

Now that Multiplier had been disarmed and was groaning on the floor, Brandy-Gavin began to Shift. His stomach shrank while his limbs grew. Auburn hair sprouted from his bald head. The stubble faded from his face. A moment later, Brandy was standing in front of me.

"Okay, I admit it," she said. "*He's* the real Gavin."

"Glad we've cleared *that* up." Trace turned on Gavin, his hands clenched into fists. "So you've been working with Vex, huh? Were you ever planning to tell me this little piece of info?"

Milton looked just as angry. "You were going to hand my best friend over to Phineas Vex?"

"How *could* you?" Sophie asked through gritted teeth.

"Everybody just calm down. . . ." Gavin staggered backward until he was up against the wall. "I can explain."

"I think you've done enough explaining already," Miranda said.

"This was the only way I could—could start the Alliance," Gavin stammered. "After what happened with the X-Treme Team, nobody would finance a new group. Then Vex came along. He offered to pay for everything. A state-of-the-art facility, uniforms, equipment. All I had to do was bring him Joshua Dread. He said he wouldn't hurt the boy. Said he needed him for something else."

"For what?" I stepped forward, glaring through the clear

divider between Gavin and me. "What did Vex want with me?"

"I d-don't know. He wouldn't tell me. I tried to convince him to leave you out of it—"

"Sure you did," Brandy scoffed. "*After* the Nameless Hero became famous."

"Fine, I confess—I saw an opportunity for you! For all of us! Is that such a bad thing? I thought I could protect you by moving you out of headquarters—away from him. At least until he sent those blasted scorpions."

"So they *were* from Vex!" I said.

Gavin nodded, frowning. "I couldn't say so at the time, but yeah—those robots were a message. Vex's way of saying, 'You can run, but you can't hide.'"

"In one of the surveillance videos, Vex said something about taking a new form," Mom said. "What was he talking about?"

Gavin's shoulders slumped, and he let out a heavy sigh. "These headquarters were never intended for training superheroes. Vex started building this place a year ago. He was going to use it as his secret lair. But after nearly dying, his plans changed. He was confined to a single room."

"The black room," I said.

"That's right. He's been in there ever since. Unable to move. Hooked up to machines that tend to his injuries. His body may have been ruined, but his mind . . . his mind is just as warped as ever. He brought in a team of experts to build him a new body. A bionic form that won't just keep him alive. It'll make him *invincible*."

My memory pitched back to the conversation I'd had with my parents over the phone about the world's best doctors, scientists, and engineers going missing.

Turning to my mom and dad, I said, "That's the secret project they were working on! They were building Vex some kind of new bionic body!"

"It all makes sense now," Dad said. "The last time we spoke, we started to tell you about one of the scientists with a tracking chip in her wristwatch."

I nodded, remembering how Elliot had eaten the phone before my parents could say where the scientist had been taken. With the insanity of the Nameless Hero's schedule, there hadn't been a chance for Mom and Dad to fill me in on the rest of the details. Until now.

"The abducted scientist," Dad said. "She was tracked back to Sheepsdale. And now I understand why. Vex was holding her in *this* underground facility, along with all his other hostages."

"How's that possible?" Sophie asked, astonished. "We never saw any sign of them."

"That's exactly what Vex had in mind," Gavin said. "He kept the doctors and scientists trapped, isolated in a separate part of the facility. Told them they wouldn't be released until they'd completed his bionic form."

A grave expression crossed Mom's face. "And when will that be?"

"Tonight. At midnight."

Dad checked the watch on his wristband. "That means we have less than an hour."

"Then we'd better move quickly," I said.

Mom stepped forward. "What do you mean *we*? I don't want you going anywhere *near* Vex."

"I'm the one Vex wants," I said, clenching my jaw. "And I want to be there when we stop him."

I could see the concern on my parents' faces, but there wasn't any time to argue. Reluctantly, they agreed that I could come along. "As long as you stay close to us," Mom insisted.

Brandy opened the holding cell, releasing everyone but Gavin. She shoved Multiplier inside and locked the cell again. With Trace and Elliot standing guard outside the cell, the rest of us set out for the black room.

Since she knew headquarters better than the rest of us, Brandy led the way. My parents jogged alongside her, their plasma pistols out and ready. I trailed behind, alongside Milton, Sophie, Miranda, and nFinity.

"Are your Gyfts working yet?" Milton asked.

Without breaking stride, I exchanged a glance with the others. Sophie's expression fixed into the look of concentration that she got whenever focusing on her power. A moment later, she shook her head. "Nothing."

nFinity and Miranda said the same.

Whatever had been in the gas that had knocked us out earlier, it was still neutralizing our powers. Even without really trying to use it, I could somehow just *tell* that my spontaneous combustion wouldn't work. It was as if something inside me had gone missing, something I hadn't noticed until it was no longer there.

We turned right and headed down a hallway that led us to the training hall where we'd fought the GLOM. We'd nearly reached the other end of the room when the door slid shut in front of us.

Brandy and my parents barely avoided colliding with the closed doorway. I barely avoided colliding with Brandy and my parents.

"Uh—what's going on?" Mom asked.

"The door," Brandy muttered, knitting her brow. "Someone must be controlling it remotely."

"But that's impossible," nFinity said. "I thought Gavin was the only one with a remote."

"He is."

"So now the doors are just closing themselves?" nFinity wondered.

"There must be someone else." Brandy's expression darkened. "Someone who can control headquarters and knows where we are right now."

My eyes turned upward. Perched in the corner, pointed right at us, was a small black surveillance camera. And with a sickening revulsion, I knew instantly who was on the other end.

"Vex," I said.

31

A shiver worked its way down my spine, the feeling you get when you're being watched. But Vex wasn't just tracking our movements. He was controlling the headquarters.

A panel in the wall opened up, spraying a burst of fire that would've roasted Milton if he hadn't ducked at the last second.

"We should probably get out of here," Milton said as smoke trailed up from his mask.

"Come on!" Brandy yelled, rushing back the way we'd come. "We'll have to find another way!"

We were halfway across the room when another section of the wall opened and three robotic lunch ladies emerged in hairnets and aprons. Except Vex must've done something to reprogram them, because now the robots didn't look like they were here to fix us a late-night snack. They had something else in mind.

"Kill! Kill! Kill!" they chanted, zooming toward us. Each had a spatula in one hand and a butcher knife in the other.

With the lightning-fast reflexes of a guy who's been in deadly situations plenty of times before, Dad reached into his utility belt and removed the small plastic container that held his remaining metal-eating ants. After opening the cap, he tossed the ants at the killer cafeteria workers.

"Ouch! Ouch! Ouch!" The robotic lunch ladies scattered across the room, trying to slap away the ants that were gnawing into their circuitry.

"This entire room is rigged with traps!" Brandy screamed.

Every surface of the training hall was designed to test our skills with deadly technology. A battering ram swung down from the ceiling, nearly taking my head off. nFinity stumbled into a pit of quicksand. He would've been buried alive if Milton hadn't pulled him out.

"As long as Vex can see us, he can keep attacking us!" Sophie yelled. "We need to take out the security cameras!"

"Shouldn't be a problem!" Mom aimed her plasma pistol and shot the two security cameras. She did the same thing to the closed door, blasting it apart bit by bit until we had an opening big enough to escape through.

"This way!" Brandy said, climbing through the opening. "We're almost out of time!"

We might have made it out of the training hall, but that didn't mean Vex was done with us yet. Buzz saws sliced through the floor like sharks' fins, chasing us down the hallway. After emerging into the next room, I staggered to a halt just in time to avoid tumbling into a stream of molten lava. The boiling red liquid gushed through a channel stretching from one wall to another.

There was only one way across. We would have to jump.

I didn't have time to contemplate whether I'd make it or not. Backing up, I gave myself a head start. Then I took off at a run and leaped. . . .

There was a moment of flinging through the air when all I could feel was the heat rising from the roiling lava beneath me.

Then I landed on the other side—but just barely. A few inches less and I would've taken a lava bath.

Sophie and Miranda jumped after me, each clearing the gap with even less room to spare.

The boiling stream of lava looked wider from this side. Another second passed before I realized why: the channel was expanding. The distance from one side to the other was steadily increasing.

nFinity charged forward, launching into the air before I could warn him. For a split second, I was sure he would plunge into the lava, but somehow he made it across. Milton would never have made it if it weren't for his jet-shoes.

By the time my parents and Brandy arrived in the room, the stream of lava had grown too wide to jump. Milton,

Miranda, Sophie, nFinity, and I inched backward to avoid falling in.

"You'll have to go on without us!" Brandy called.

I stared across the widening gap separating us from the adults. "Isn't there some other way?"

"Not if you want to stop Vex by midnight!" Brandy said.

"You can do it!" Mom's voice was firm. Her eyes never left mine. "You have to."

"Here—take this." Dad tossed his plasma pistol. It landed on the other side and skidded across the floor. nFinity bent down to pick it up.

"The black room is that way!" Brandy pointed toward an arched doorway. "Into the next room, then turn right."

Her directions led us to the long corridor that I'd been down once before with Miranda. Except this time, instead of avoiding the security cameras that lined the walls, we raced past them. The clatter of our pounding footsteps echoed in my ears.

We came to a stop in front of the black door.

The idea of facing down Vex had been a lot easier to grasp when I'd thought my parents would be there with me. But now it was just us—five kids in uniforms. No superpowers, no utility belts. All we had was Dad's plasma pistol. Would that be enough?

I pushed all my doubts away. Once Vex got his new bionic body, he'd be invincible. And unless we managed to stop him in the next three minutes, that was exactly what was going to happen.

Lost in these thoughts, I didn't notice nFinity turning

and raising the plasma pistol, until the barrel was pointed right at my chest.

"Any sudden moves and I pull the trigger," he said.

I felt like I'd stumbled into a bizarre dream. None of this made any sense. nFinity stepped forward calmly, a dark grin forming on his face.

"Everybody back up." He jabbed the plasma pistol, forcing us backward until we were against the wall. His eyes narrowed behind his mask.

"Wh-what're you doing?" Miranda asked in a wounded voice. "Vex is going to be here any minute."

"That's right. And I imagine he'll be pretty happy to see what I brought him."

Milton gaped at nFinity, his mouth hanging open. "You and Vex—you're working together?"

nFinity shook his head. "Not yet. But I've been in this business long enough to know that it's never too late to form new partnerships. It's an opportunity too good to pass up, really. I give Vex something he wants"—nFinity's eyes flickered over to me—"and he gets rid of the competition."

"What're you talking about?" I asked.

"Isn't it obvious? Ever since the world found out about the Nameless Hero, I've been ignored, overlooked. *I* was supposed to be the cover story of *Super Scoop*. *I* was supposed to be the one with endorsement deals. But then you came along." nFinity glared at me. "Do you have any idea how hard I worked to get where I am? I'm not about to let you swoop in and take my place."

I struggled to comprehend what I was hearing. So there'd been some truth to *Super Scoop*'s claims of a power struggle between us. I just hadn't known about it.

"Don't act so surprised, Nameless! You want the attention more than any of us. Back at the commercial shoot when those scorpions attacked, you stood back and let those things overpower us. You watched while I nearly got killed."

My memory flashed with the sight of nFinity, blood streaming out of multiple wounds, cornered by scorpions. "I wanted to fight sooner," I said. "But Gavin . . . he was holding me back."

nFinity shook his head furiously. "Don't blame this on anyone else. It was *you*! You were waiting for just the right moment—until the rest of us were weak. Nearly defeated. The perfect moment for the Nameless Hero to swoop in and save the day."

"You have to believe me," I pleaded. "That wasn't the way it happened."

"Shut up!" nFinity's finger tightened on the trigger. "Because of you, I'm nothing. What am I supposed to do now? Perform in shopping malls, showing off my fire tricks for six-year-olds? I don't think so. Once Vex takes care of the Nameless Hero, things will go back to the way they were. I'll be famous again."

My heart thundered in my ears. In the corner of my vision, I could see the black door. Vex was behind there. Any second now, he'd be unstoppable.

Until now, Sophie had taken nFinity's sudden betrayal in silence. But I could see in her face that it hit her the hardest.

"nFinity, please," she pleaded, her voice wavering. "You're not thinking clearly. This isn't who you are."

"I'm sorry, Sophie." nFinity's expression softened, and just for a second I saw the cool, good-looking hero Sophie had adored all this time. But it was only a moment. Then his face changed again. His jaw clenched in fierce determination. "This is the way it has to be."

My brain seared with the hopelessness of the situation. I didn't know what was worse—getting blasted by the plasma pistol or waiting around for Vex to show up. Unfortunately, I didn't have much choice. A thunderous noise rumbled through the corridor. Something was moving behind the black door. Something enormous.

I glanced at my friends. Was this the last time I was ever going to see them?

"I'm the one Vex wants," I said to nFinity. "Not them. Let the others go."

"Not a chance." nFinity's lip curled into a sneer that wiped away any last trace of the teenage superhero he'd once been. "I can't have any witnesses contradicting my side of the story."

The floor trembled beneath my feet. The walls shook.

"Sounds like the guest of honor is on his way," nFinity said.

All at once, the black door shattered into a thousand

pieces. The wall around it crumbled. I covered my face to block the flying debris. Opening my eyes again, I saw a figure emerging from the black room.

Phineas Vex had arrived. And by the looks of it, he'd gotten a major upgrade.

32

I'd thought Vex was pretty terrifying when he was just an old dude with a cane, but that was nothing compared to the way he looked now. He towered over the rest of us, a mountain of armor-plated muscles and devious gadgetry.

The only part of Vex that was still visible was his face, leering through a clear window in the head of his bionic capsule. A patchwork of grisly scars crisscrossed his skin. One of his eyes was white and unseeing. The other stared cruelly down at me.

From the neck down, Vex was sealed away inside a ten-foot-tall body that made even the bulkiest bodybuilder look like a weakling by comparison. His massive arms and legs looked as if they'd been formed from solid titanium, and his chest bulged like an indestructible tank.

Vex stomped forward, each step shaking the ground.

More and more of the walls crumbled down around him. He must've still been getting used to the suit, because his movements were stiff and jerky, like those of a toddler just learning to walk.

"I've waited a long time to meet you again, Joshua Dread." Vex's voice boomed from a speaker built into his new high-tech body. His eyes passed over Sophie, Milton, and Miranda. "And how polite of you to bring your friends along."

"I—I captured them, sir," nFinity said. "I wouldn't let them destroy you."

"Glad to see you've had a change of heart," Vex replied. "Your service won't be overlooked. Especially if you stay on my side."

A dark look of satisfaction formed on nFinity's face. "I will do anything, sir."

"After so long in that miserable dark room, I can finally move again." Vex held out one bionic arm, looking it over admiringly. "I've been waiting for months to test out my new body. And now's my chance."

Vex grabbed hold of Milton's arm so quickly that none of us even had the chance to flinch.

"As you can see, the limbs have excellent precision and speed." Vex lifted Milton off the ground. "And just wait till I show you the added features. I'm able to detect every physical characteristic of those around me—every strength and weakness, all with a simple body scan."

To demonstrate, a panel opened up in the chest of Vex's

robo-suit, and a grid of red lasers traced up and down Milton's body.

A moment later, Vex recited the results of the scan: "Above-average agility but your speed suffers in long distances due to a broken leg when you were nine. Type A blood. No discernible Gyfts. And you really should floss more regularly."

"Lemme go!" Milton squirmed and kicked, but Vex's grip didn't falter.

"I had my team of scientists analyze the powers of the most fearsome supervillains on earth and distill each and every one of them into a function of this suit." Vex turned his one good eye on me. "Including your mother's."

With his free hand, Vex motioned to the ceiling. A rumbling sound grew louder above him until a thick brown root burst through the ceiling panel. Another broke through an instant later. Like tentacles, the roots extended farther into the corridor, wrapping around Sophie and Miranda, lifting them off the ground.

I realized at once what Vex meant. His bionic body allowed him to control plant life, just like my mom.

Sophie and Miranda clutched at the roots, kicking in the air. But there was no escaping.

Vex's magnified voice boomed across this horrible scene. "But unlike your mother, I'm not limited to only *one* power. Surely you're aware of the way Revoltor can levitate objects in thin air. Well, now so can I. . . ."

Vex released Milton. But instead of falling, Milton

drifted in front of him, as if he were suspended by invisible wires.

"I'm capable of generating an electric charge like Tesla the Terrible." Vex flicked his fingers, and a tiny bolt of lightning zapped Milton's arm.

"Ouch!" Milton screamed, recoiling from the shock.

"And like Raven Fury, I can use mind-control to attack others." Vex narrowed his one good eye, focusing on Sophie, Miranda, and Milton, who were dangling in front of him—two held up by the roots, the other floating in midair. And all of a sudden, my friends clutched at their throats, as if they were being choked by some unseen force.

"As you can see, there's no point in resisting. I am now indestructible. And it's all thanks to you, Joshua Dread." Vex's terrible gaze turned back to me. "You nearly killed me the last time we faced each other. But I survived. And now I'm stronger than I've ever been before. Reborn as the greatest supervillain the world has ever known."

Horror rippled through my entire body. My friends struggled in front of me. If someone didn't stop Vex soon, they would choke to death. Beside me, nFinity was watching with a look of sinister fascination on his face.

"Let them go!" I screamed at Vex. "I'll do whatever you want! Just let my friends live!"

"Not a chance," Vex said. "Your friends were there the night that I nearly died. They also bear responsibility. The only reason I'm sparing your life is because I have something much bigger in store for you."

I clenched my hands into fists, plunging my mind deep

into concentration. If I could just trigger my spontaneous combustion, maybe I could fight back, do something to stop Vex, to make him release my friends. Gritting my teeth, I focused harder. And for a second, I thought it might actually be working. A sudden *WHOOSH* rushed through my ears. But it wasn't my Gyft. It was something else. Some-*one* else.

"Release your evil grip on those children, you fiend!"

I whirled around, and my heart leaped at the sight of Captain Justice flying through the corridor, his shiny blue cape sweeping behind him. And he wasn't alone either. A reality-TV crew trailed him—two cameramen and a guy with a boom mic buzzing through the air in jet packs—recording everything.

"Engage Spear of Freedom!" A holographic blue spear appeared from the bulky metal band around Captain Justice's wrist. He thrust it forward. A flash of blue erupted in front of me as the spear collided with Vex.

I'd seen Captain Justice's hologram weapons cause some major damage to my parents over the years, but the Spear of Freedom didn't even make a dent in Vex's armor.

"I'll deal with you children once I've finished off Captain Justice," Vex said, turning his attention away from Sophie, Miranda, and Milton. All at once, his power over them vanished. Milton fell suddenly. The roots untangled from Sophie and Miranda. They dropped to the floor next to Milton, gasping to regain their breath.

"I'm pleased to see you brought your camera crew, Justice," Vex growled. "Now the entire world will have

CAPTAIN JUSTICE

Captain Justice has battled fearsome villains, starred in million-dollar marketing campaigns, and appeared on the covers of countless magazines. And now he's adding a new accomplishment to his career: reality-TV star.

a chance to witness your death. You see, my suit wasn't outfitted only to replicate the powers of villains. I've also had it designed to match the abilities of one particular superhero—*you*."

As Vex spoke, a bazooka rose behind his back.

"Engage Rocket Launcher of Hatred!" Vex bellowed.

And like the hologram weapons that appeared from Captain Justice's wristbands, the bazooka launched a red holographic rocket. I barely had a chance to dive to the side before it blasted across the corridor, spiraling in Captain Justice's direction.

"Watch out!" Captain Justice shoved his cameramen out of the way. The rocket flew past them. "You can attack me if you want, Vex," Captain Justice yelled. "But leave my reality-TV crew out of it."

Out of the corner of my eye, I caught sight of nFinity raising the plasma pistol and taking aim at Captain Justice. I dove just in time to tackle nFinity before he could get the shot off. With chaos roaring all around me, I tried to wrestle the pistol away from nFinity, but he overpowered me. One hand gripped my neck. The other raised the plasma pistol.

"Hope you've enjoyed your fifteen minutes of fame, Nameless Hero," nFinity snarled. "Because you're about to become the *Faceless* Hero."

He aimed the pistol between my eyes.

"NO!" Vex screamed. "I need him alive!"

nFinity's eyes burned, but he didn't dare disobey Vex's order. I took advantage of his hesitation to kick him away from me. nFinity sprawled onto his back, and I scrambled away.

"Engage Smoke Screen of Integrity!" Captain Justice yelled.

A blue cloud burst from his wristband, filling the corridor. It was like I'd suddenly gone blind. All I could see was blue. I staggered away from Vex, until the dim outline of Captain Justice emerged from the cloud. He had Sophie, Miranda, and Milton under one arm. I could see the vague shapes of the camera crew around him.

"Engage Protective Umbrella of Virtue!" Captain Justice said.

A flash of blue cut through the cloud as he slammed the umbrella sideways, creating a barrier between us and Vex.

"Come along," Captain Justice said. "The umbrella won't hold him off forever."

I stumbled alongside Captain Justice and the others. Behind me, an ominous voice boomed from somewhere in the cloud.

"This isn't over!" Phineas Vex sounded like he was speaking from nowhere and everywhere at the same time. "I'll find you, Joshua Dread. Soon, I'll find you!"

The ground trembled beneath my feet as Vex's massive footsteps shook the corridor. For a horrifying instant, I was sure he was following us. But the heavy stomping was moving in the other direction, joined by smaller footsteps that must've been nFinity's. Soon the sounds disappeared entirely and the blue cloud began to clear.

"Great job back there with the hologram umbrella

thingy," one of the cameramen said to Captain Justice. "You sure we can't try to get one more take? I missed the shot with all the blue smoke."

"I'm afraid not, Kenny," Captain Justice said. "We're lucky to get away in the first place. The only reason my tactic worked is because Vex is still getting used to his bionic body. I fear that there won't be any stopping him once he's mastered all the functions."

Keeping up a quick pace as he led us back to my parents and Brandy, Captain Justice explained how he'd found headquarters. He'd been tracking Vex for years, ever since Vex had killed his wife. Not long ago, Captain Justice had picked up suspicious activity that could only be linked back to Vex. A huge underground facility. Scientists being forced to design a suit that wouldn't just keep a man alive but would turn him into an all-powerful being. Even a strange rumor that the new superhero group the Alliance of the Impossible was somehow connected.

"Of course, I was busy shooting *Hangin' with Justice*, not to mention my usual schedule of kicking villainous butt and saving the world," Captain Justice said. "But when I discovered the headquarters, I came here right away—"

"Yeah, we were in the middle of shooting a romantic dinner with Scarlett Flame," said one of the cameramen. "You could've at least given us some warning that you'd have to interrupt your date. We missed out on a lot of good footage—"

"Wait a minute," Sophie looked up at her dad with shock. "You're *dating*?"

Captain Justice came to a stop, turning to face Sophie. "I should've told you sooner. It's just . . . with what happened to your mother, I didn't know how you'd take it."

"If you're dating again, it's fine. I just wish you'd *tell* me."

Meanwhile, the TV crew was inching closer on all sides. One camera trained on Captain Justice, the other on Sophie. The boom mic dangled between them, picking up all their dialogue.

"I'm sorry, honey," Captain Justice said.

"It's okay," Sophie replied. "I'm just glad you showed up when you did."

"This is great stuff," one of the cameramen said under his breath.

It looked like Sophie and Captain Justice were about to hug. The crew was just moving in for the close-up on the big emotional scene, when Milton burst in front of one camera.

"What's Scarlett Flame like?" Milton was hopping up and down excitedly. "Does her power medallion really let her see into the future?"

The cameraman cursed quietly to himself.

"Are you and Scarlett Flame really dating?" Milton persisted. "'Cause that would be awesome!"

Captain Justice actually seemed to be blushing. "Ms. Flame is a . . . uh—very charming and . . . er—talented superhero lady," he spluttered.

"You really like her, huh?" Sophie gave her dad a playful punch on the shoulder.

Meanwhile, Milton was tugging on Captain Justice's

cape to get his attention. "A few weeks ago, *Super Scoop* reported that Scarlett Flame inherited her power from her grandmother. Is that true? Can a superpower skip a generation, or could it be that—"

"We should keep moving." Captain Justice began walking again hurriedly. "No telling what dangers are still lurking in this facility."

I think he just wanted to change the subject.

33

"This is kind of awkward."

Sophie was standing beside me, watching her dad attempt to make conversation with my parents. It wasn't the first time they'd met. Captain Justice and the Dread Duo had fought each other plenty of times over the years. And then—once they'd discovered that their kids hung out together—the three of them had formed some sort of unspoken truce.

But now there were cameramen around. And that weird fuzzy microphone hanging over them. And in the past, whenever cameras were focused on Captain Justice and the Dread Duo, it was because they were trying to kill each other.

My mom kept glancing at the cameras like they were going to bite her. Dad looked like he wanted to swat the fuzzy microphone out of the air like a volleyball.

"I think my parents are worried about what'll happen to their reputation," I said. "It's been a while since their last evil scheme. I'm not sure how the rest of the supervillain community will like seeing them chat with Captain Justice."

"Sounds like *Hangin' with Justice* might be worth watching after all," Sophie said with a smile.

We were in Smoothie Sensations, traveling back up to the surface of the earth. After meeting with my parents and Brandy, we'd found everyone else where we'd left them. Gavin and Multiplier still locked in the holding cell. Trace and Elliot standing guard outside. Except there'd been a new guest at the party: Captain Justice's robot butler, Stanley. Captain Justice had reached headquarters by drilling half a mile into the earth in a custom-made pod that only Stanley could operate. They'd left the pod in headquarters to hitch a ride with us and make sure we made it back to the surface safely. On the way, Gavin had guided us to the room where Vex was keeping his hostages—a dozen doctors, scientists, and engineers who looked like they hadn't slept in weeks.

And now there we were. Superheroes and supervillains. A reality-TV camera crew. A bunch of skittish men and women in lab coats. And not one but *two* robot butlers.

"I bet Stanley and Elliot have a lot to talk about," Sophie observed, looking across the crowded smoothie shop at the two of them.

"I wouldn't be so sure about that," I said.

Stanley was tall and slim, dressed in a spotless black

jacket and matching bow tie. Next to him, Elliot looked even more like a trash can than usual.

"Do you perform all the driving duties for the Dreads as well?" Stanley asked in his precise electronic voice.

"Mrs. Dread not let me near the caaaaaar since I try to eat the bummmmper," Elliot slurred.

"I see." Stanley ran a silver hand along the lapel of his jacket. "And I presume you do all the cooking?"

"I maked meat loooaaaaf, but the kitchen catched fiiiire."

"I can't believe *he* saved *your* life," Milton said. He and Miranda were standing a few feet away, making smoothies.

"A few more strawberries," Miranda suggested.

Milton dumped a scoopful of frozen strawberries into the blender, added some ice, and hit the button marked DELUXE.

Once the smoothies had been poured, Miranda handed me a cup. "So you got Elliot's attention by ringing some kind of a bell?"

"The Liberty Bell," I said, thinking back to the way he'd burst into the tanning salon. "I guess it's a good thing my parents kept Elliot after all."

The TV crew made their way in our direction. All of a sudden, the boom mic was hanging between the four of us. Cameras circled like giant insects.

My shoulders tightened. How were we supposed to have a normal conversation *now*? I reminded myself that it wasn't *me* that people would be watching on their TVs.

It was the Nameless Hero. Along with Supersonic, Firefly, and Prodigy—four fifths of the Alliance of the Impossible.

The only one missing was nFinity. It was still strange to think that he was gone. Vanished into the smoke with Phineas Vex. Nobody was more shaken by his betrayal than Sophie. In her eyes was a mixture of sadness and disappointment at what he'd done.

The TV crew seemed to be having a stifling effect on all of us. Hopefully they'd cut this scene. I'd feel sorry for anyone who tuned in to see four junior superheroes just standing around, sipping their smoothies.

When Milton finally spoke up, he was like a different person. Maybe he was nervous, or maybe he just wanted to seem especially heroic for the cameras. Either way, he puffed out his chest and spoke in this weird extra-loud voice.

"Well, that sure was a thrilling adventure we had, pals!"

Milton gestured with his arms grandly, like he was giving a speech to an auditorium full of people, not chatting with a few friends. He glanced at one of the cameras, cleared his throat, then continued:

"We faced many setbacks and . . . er—nearly got killed by some robotic lunch ladies, but in the end we prevailed."

I could see Sophie struggling to keep a straight face. Miranda looked like she was on the verge of laughing too.

Strangely enough, this was almost what I'd imagined my summer would be like. At least in some ways. Hanging out with friends. Staying up way past my bedtime. Getting brain freeze from drinking my smoothie too quickly.

I just had to try to ignore the fact that I was being filmed by a reality-TV crew while wearing shiny tights. Or that the smoothie shop was actually a secret elevator carrying us from an underground facility. And of course, my best friend had suddenly started acting like some kind of mini Captain Justice.

So, not *exactly* what I'd had in mind.

"Let us raise our smoothies!" Milton boomed, lifting his cup. "In celebration of good triumphing over evil. And to being such super friends. Get it—*super*? And of course, vanquishing our foe, even though he had a really amazing robotic suit with a built-in hologram bazooka—"

Sophie jabbed him with her elbow.

"Anyway, cheers," Milton completed.

I raised my cup, and so did the others.

"Cheers!"

I stepped through the front door of Smoothie Sensations and into the parking lot. Overhead lights glowed in the darkness. Scientists and doctors milled around, looking relieved to be above ground again. It was past two in the morning, but my mind still buzzed with leftover adrenaline. I guess Captain Justice's armored SUV was still in the shop, because I caught sight of his black limousine nearby.

"What should we do with these two?" Mom asked, nodding toward Multiplier and Gavin, who were shackled in a pair of my dad's titanium handcuffs.

"I've already notified the authorities of their capture," Captain Justice said. "The FBI is waiting for me to drop them off at the local courthouse. Perhaps it's better if you don't come along for that part."

"You might have a point," Dad said. "I believe we're still near the top of that pesky Most Wanted list."

Captain Justice shoved Gavin and Multiplier into the back of his limo. "Don't get used to this," he said to them. "After tonight, you two won't be riding in one of these for a long time." He turned to Multiplier. "And if you even *think* about cloning yourself, there won't be anything left for you to multiply. Got it?"

Multiplier nodded dejectedly. Gavin wasn't planning to go out so quietly, though.

"All I wanted to do was put a team together again!" he hollered. His eyes flashed wildly over the parking lot until they settled where I was standing next to Sophie, Miranda, and Milton. "I gave you everything! A state-of-the-art facility! Professional training! Working with Vex was the only way. Without me, you would be nothing! I made you FAMOUS!"

His speech came to an end when Captain Justice slammed the door shut.

"Is your Gyft still disabled?" I asked Miranda.

She nodded. "Yep. Why?"

"I was just thinking—if you had your superpowered intuition back, you might know whether we were ever going to see each other again."

"Oh, I don't need my Gyft for that."

"What d'you mean?"

"My mom already signed me up for school in Sheepsdale." Miranda smiled. "I'll probably have to travel to auditions on weekends, and my mom's already looking for tutors who can work with me after school on kickboxing and mind reading."

I chuckled. "Typical extracurricular activities."

After excusing myself from the other kids, I made my way toward Brandy, who was standing alone in the glow of an overhead lamp.

"Crazy night, huh?" I said.

An exhausted smile passed across Brandy's lips. "You could say that."

"Will you and Trace be okay? I mean, now that Gavin's going to jail?"

"We'll be fine. Won't be the first time a superhero team falls apart on us." All of a sudden, Brandy got very serious. She peered down at me like she was searching my face for clues. "Do you remember what Gavin said about the headquarters? That it wasn't originally intended for training superheroes?"

"Yeah. Gavin said Vex was going to use it for his secret lair or something."

"Well, when I was searching Gavin's office, I stumbled across some of Vex's old documents from before the headquarters had been built. There was a specific reason why Vex wanted his lair in Sheepsdale."

I glanced across the parking lot at Tantastic, reminded of the futuristic facility a half mile beneath my feet. From the moment our bus first came to a stop in this parking lot, it had struck me as strange that the Gyfted & Talented headquarters was located in Sheepsdale, so close to where I lived. It had seemed like an impossible coincidence.

"Really? What is it?" I asked.

Brandy hesitated, as if considering whether to go on. "There's something here," she said finally. "Something in Sheepsdale that Vex was after."

"What?"

"A weapon of some kind. Vex seemed to think it held the key to taking over the world."

I looked around, confused. "And he thought he could find that in a shopping center?"

Brandy didn't crack a smile. "I wasn't able to find out any more. But I thought you should at least know. Now that Vex has taken his new form, he'll most likely be looking for it again."

And that wasn't the only thing he'd be searching for. My mind pitched back to the smoky corridor and Vex's parting words. *I'll find you, Joshua Dread. Soon, I'll find you!*

"I know this must be difficult." Brandy brought her hand down on my shoulder. "But just remember—you're a lot stronger than you think."

I was still trying to figure out what she meant by that

when Brandy turned to go. "Goodbye, Joshua. And good luck."

The air shimmered, and Trace appeared beside her. Instead of his usual smirk, he actually shot me a halfway sincere-looking smile. "So long, kid."

And the two of them walked off into the hazy night together.

34

We made up our minds to stay in Sheepsdale. It wasn't an easy decision. With an invincible bionic billionaire out there looking for me, my parents' first instinct was to pack our belongings, change our identities, and start a new life somewhere else. But the more we thought about it, that began to seem like an even bigger risk. If there really was some kind of superweapon in Sheepsdale, we couldn't let Vex get to it.

And there was also Captain Justice. Even though my parents had a complicated relationship with the superhero (and that was putting it lightly), we all shared a common enemy: Phineas Vex. When the time came to face Vex again, we knew we would only stand a chance of defeating him if we stuck together.

"I can't believe we're actually staying in Sheepsdale

because of Captain Justice," Dad said, shaking his head in wonderment.

Whatever the reason, I was just happy to be staying. For the first time in my life, I had a real group of friends. Milton, Sophie—and now Miranda. And with Gyfted & Talented coming to an early end, we had the rest of the summer to spend together.

Back at home, I was hoping everything would settle back to normal. Or as close to normal as possible when you live with a couple of supervillains. But there was just one little thing standing in the way of that.

I was still the most famous kid on earth.

After failing to show up for a few dozen of the interviews and photo shoots that Gavin had scheduled for me, websites and TV shows started asking, "What's happened to the Nameless Hero?"

All kinds of crazy rumors circulated on the Internet. I tried to ignore them, which wasn't so easy when Milton kept emailing me links to articles and blog posts. I usually deleted them right away, but I couldn't help catching the headlines:

Did the Nameless Hero Perish in a Volcanic Eruption???

Superkid Dragged Away to Ultra-Private Mental Institution for Celebs!!!

Nameless Spotted in Cancun, Sunbathing in Sombrero

Super Scoop ran another cover story about me the next week. Underneath a photo of me posing in my uniform and mask was a bold caption:

"You're never gonna believe what she wrote!" Milton flapped the magazine in my face.

I'd gone over to his house to play video games—not read *Super Scoop*. I wasn't too interested in finding out what Cosgrove had to say about me this time. But Milton wouldn't let the subject drop.

He flipped the magazine open. "It says here you were kidnapped!"

"Oh, that's a new one." I rolled my eyes. "And who do they think kidnapped me?"

"The Dread Duo!"

I dropped my controller. "They think that . . . my parents kidnapped me?"

"Yeah. Except—well . . . they don't know that *you're* you. Or that your parents are your parents. The article says an eyewitness spotted the Nameless Hero in the backseat of a Volvo that was being driven by the Dread Duo. I guess they figured you were their hostage."

"It must've been the night we drove back from Smoothie Sensations. We were all so tired—nobody bothered changing out of their uniforms."

"It gets worse from there." Milton read out loud from the article: "'An inside source claims that the rest of the Alliance of the Impossible has gone into hiding, afraid that they'll be next to fall victim to the nefarious plans of Dr. Dread and his despicable wife, the Botanist. For now, it seems that the Nameless Hero has gone from five-star hotels to an extended stay in the Dreads' dungeon of doom.'"

"I can't believe they can print this stuff!" I reached for the magazine.

"Hey, this is a collector's edition!" Milton held the copy of *Super Scoop* protectively. "Anyway, it's not *all* bad. There's this other article that lists overrated superheroes. And they ranked nFinity as the most overhyped supercelebrity of the year."

nFinity. Nobody had heard or seen anything from him since the night he'd betrayed us. According to *Super Scoop,* he was hiding out from my parents (*and* was overrated). But we knew the truth. He was out there somewhere with Phineas Vex. And I had a bad feeling we'd be seeing both of them again someday.

A few days later, a commercial on TV caught my attention.

"Tune in for the special two-hour premiere of *Hangin' with Justice* this Thursday!" The voice blared from the TV's speakers while images of Captain Justice flashed on the screen. "In a very special first episode, we reveal what went down between Nameless Hero, nFinity, and the rest of the Alliance of the Impossible."

I guess I shouldn't have been too surprised. The camera crew had been there on the night Captain Justice had saved us from Vex. It's not like they were going to just throw that footage away. But I wasn't sure whether I actually wanted to watch any of it. The entire experience had been nerve-racking enough the first time. Did I really want to go through it again on TV?

"Of course you should!" Milton exclaimed when I told him I was having doubts. "It's our reality-TV debut!"

"But we already know what happens. Don't you think that'll be boring?"

"This is reality TV. Nothing's boring. Besides, there's something else you should probably know. . . ." Milton hesitated, examining his fingernails.

"What?"

"I kind of—uh . . . told Sophie and Miranda that we could watch it at your place."

At first, I assumed Milton was joking. He knew about my parents' no-visitors policy. Just because he'd been allowed in my replica bedroom didn't mean my parents were going to let him see the real thing.

But Milton kept insisting, and so later that day I brought it up with my parents. And big surprise—they weren't too thrilled about the possibility.

"What happens if one of your friends wanders down into the basement where I keep the zombies?" Mom asked in an exasperated voice. "It would be a little awkward to explain to another set of parents that their kid's brain has been eaten during your playdate."

"First of all, nobody says 'playdate' anymore," I began. "And we can warn them ahead of time about the basement."

Mom shook her head. "Still. I don't think it's a good idea."

"It's only Milton, Sophie, and Miranda. They know about you guys already. They've met you guys. So what's the big deal if they see where we live?"

"Why can't you do it at one of their houses?" Dad asked.

"Milton's mom is hosting her book club that night. Captain Justice and Stanley are going to some kind of big party for the premiere of the show, so we can't do it there. And Miranda's still getting moved into her place."

Mom and Dad considered this for a moment. Even though I hadn't really wanted to watch the episode to begin with, I was crossing my fingers that they'd say yes. The more I thought about it, the more unfair it seemed that my parents had never allowed me to have a single friend over. No sleepovers. No after-school video games. Nothing.

This was a chance to change all that. A way to feel like a normal kid with normal parents (even if we *did* have to warn my friends about the zombies beneath the floorboards).

"You weren't exactly *truthful* with us about your summer plans," Dad reminded me.

"Especially the part about becoming a superhero," Mom added.

"Or a world-famous celebrity."

The two of them exchanged a glance. I noticed the hint of a smile at the corner of my mom's mouth.

"But I suppose it *is* a special occasion," she said.

"So we're going to allow it," Dad went on. "*This* time."

A huge smile stretched across my face. "Thanks, guys!"

I jogged out of the room before they could change their minds.

35

ophie was the first to show up. I felt a squirm of embarrassment as she walked into our house. Sophie and Captain Justice lived in a mansion with more rooms than you could count. Everything was state-of-the-art and glistening. *And* they had a robot butler to bring us whatever we wanted.

My house was another story. The rooms felt crammed with my dad's half-finished inventions and my mom's experiments. And thanks to Elliot's "cleaning," it looked like a tornado had recently swept through the place. Holes in the walls. Three-legged chairs. Busted lamps.

"Sorry it's such a mess," I muttered, showing Sophie into the living room.

"Are you kidding?" Sophie looked around, wide-eyed. "I love it! Your house actually looks like a *house*. Like someone really lives here."

"Um . . . yeah. I guess."

"Every house I've ever lived in has felt like a hotel. Like a really big hotel and we're the first guests who've ever stayed there. The furniture all goes unused. Half the rooms are empty. And my dad's never around anyway."

Sophie wandered from the living room to the dining room. A broken circuit board was lying on the table, surrounded by a bunch of my dad's tools. In the corner was Micus—

"And you have houseplants!" Sophie gushed, her eyes landing on the mutant ficus.

"Actually," I warned, "that particular houseplant—"

"I've always wanted plants," Sophie interrupted, too caught up to listen. "But my dad says he's allergic. Is that even a thing? Can someone be *allergic* to houseplants?"

Sophie took a step toward the mutant ficus. Alarm bells went off in my head. I'd been attacked by Micus so often that I avoided this entire *side* of the dining room. And why was Micus just sitting there? It made me think of a predator waiting for the right moment to strike. . . .

"Uh . . . Sophie." I rushed forward. "That's not a normal plant! You should probably—"

Too late. When Sophie reached out to touch one of Micus's leaves, the mutant made its move.

And started doing tricks for her.

Sophie clapped in amazement as the ficus began dancing—its branches flailing from side to side. Afterward, it picked up a few clods of soil and juggled them.

"I see you've met Micus," Mom said, entering the room.

Sophie turned to my mom, smiling. "Did you create that?"

"I did indeed. The world's first plant that can control its own movements, understand human speech—"

"And attack people," I murmured.

"What are you talking about?" Sophie petted one of Micus's leaves. "It looks gentle to me."

"Maybe now, but I'm telling you, that plant's dangerous. He's tried to kill me. Multiple times."

Sophie gave me a look like she was trying to decide whether I was kidding or not.

"If you'd like, I can show you a few other plants I'm working on," Mom said.

Sophie eagerly followed my mom out of the room. As soon as they turned their backs, a big clump of soil smacked me right in the face.

Miranda and Milton arrived a little later. As we all settled in the living room, I could tell that I wasn't the only one who was nervous having guests over. Mom and Dad weren't used to being hosts either.

"Does everyone have everything they need?" Dad asked.

"We're fine," I said.

"If you'd like to sit closer to the television, I upgraded the sofas so they're remote-control-operated—"

"Seriously, we're *fine*, Dad!"

Mom poked her head through the doorway. "How about

some drinks, kids? We have water, caffeinated cola, non-caffeinated cola, lemonade, fruit juice, homemade condensed vegetable blend. . . ."

Meanwhile, Elliot was wandering through the room. A serving tray wobbled in his hands.

"I have cooked snaaaaacks!"

"Sure, I'll take some," Milton said.

Elliot handed Milton a plate. "Buffalo wiiiiiings!"

Milton stared down at the plate. The buffalo wings looked more like deep-fried worms. "Uh . . . thanks," he said, setting the plate down as far away as possible.

Miranda leaned toward me. "Thanks for having me over."

"I'm just glad you can stay in Sheepsdale," I said. "It'll be fun having one more Gyfted kid around school."

"By the way, you might want to move to another seat."

"What do you mean?"

"Just trust me."

Taking her word for it, I switched over to the recliner. And I was just in time too. A second later, Elliot tripped over the rug and the serving tray flipped out of his grip. A pile of fried blobs landed right where I'd just been sitting.

We were still figuring out refreshments and living room configuration when the show started. *Hangin' with Justice* followed Captain Justice through his everyday life—eating breakfast, exercising at the gym, getting a haircut. Scenes of him appearing on other TV shows. Business meetings. Photo shoots.

"People think superheroes are constantly battling super-villains, but there's a lot more to it than that," Captain Justice said while getting a manicure.

Sophie groaned.

We also got to see Captain Justice's response to Multiplier's pranks. He joined efforts to clear all the purple Jell-O out of the Grand Canyon and scrub the graffiti off Mount Rushmore.

"The authorities are still looking for the other letters of the Hollywood sign," Captain Justice said to the camera. "So at the moment, it still reads 'LOL.' Which I assume is some kind of devious code to other supervillains of the world."

Scarlett Flame showed up a few times in the show, her long red hair flowing halfway down her back and her golden body armor fitting her like a one-piece swimsuit. Since she was the most famous female superhero in the country, I'd seen her plenty of times before. But never like this. Whenever she got around Captain Justice, the two of them flirted like a couple of teenagers. Captain Justice usually acted so authoritative and bombastic, but as soon as Scarlett Flame was nearby, he suddenly became nervous, mixing up his words and fiddling with his armor-plated wristbands.

"They totally like each other!" Milton exclaimed, scooting forward on the couch.

Sophie covered her eyes, as if she were watching a horror movie, not a reality show.

And then I showed up on-screen, dressed as the Nameless Hero. Sophie, Milton, and Miranda were nearby in the shot.

It was like returning to the scene of a nightmare. All of a sudden, I was back in the corridor. Seeing nFinity's icy gaze, as he waited for us to die. And Vex looming over everyone else in his bionic suit.

Only after Captain Justice rescued us could I relax and feel embarrassed about how sweaty and nervous I looked whenever the cameras got close.

As I watched my friends and me standing around in our uniforms, I thought maybe it hadn't been such a bad start to the summer after all. Sure, we nearly got killed a bunch of times. And becoming famous hadn't been quite as great as I'd thought it would be. But we all made it out alive, and the Nameless Hero had gone into early retirement.

I looked at the others sitting around me. We weren't superheroes any longer, but at least we were still friends.

Once the show was over, Miranda's mom came by to drive Sophie and Miranda home. Meanwhile, Milton was putting all his effort into convincing my parents to let him spend the night.

"After being banned from coming over for the past three years, we have lots of catching up to do," Milton explained. "I was thinking, five slumber parties a week for the rest of the summer."

My parents gave Milton their most supervillainous glares.

"Uh . . . on—on second thought," Milton spluttered. "How about just tonight?"

"Very well," Dad agreed. "You can stay over tonight."

"Wahooooooo!"

Milton ran home to get his things. When he got back to my room, he was lugging a Captain Justice–themed duffel bag stuffed with junk food, sodas, and video games.

"And look what else I brought." Milton reached into the duffel and removed a lump of spandex material, along with a mask and a pair of bulky red jet-boots. "My uniform!"

"I thought we were done with all that," I said.

"Aw, come on! It's not like we're gonna go out and fight crime. I just thought we could take a little spin around Sheepsdale. Didn't you keep your uniform?"

"Yeah, but—"

"Awesome! This is gonna be so much fun!"

I glanced toward my closet, where my uniform was folded next to the laundry hamper. Maybe the Nameless Hero wasn't quite as retired as I'd thought.

After changing into our uniforms, Milton and I tip-toed downstairs, carrying our boots to make less noise. We made our way through the living room, into the dining room (luckily, Micus was sleeping), and then the kitchen. After opening the door to the garage, I flipped on the light. There in the corner were the hover scooters.

"Ahem!"

Clutching my chest, I spun around as if I expected to

see Multiplier behind me. But it was even worse than that. It was my mom. She was standing in the middle of the kitchen, her arms crossed sternly.

We were so busted. Sneaking out at night was bad enough. But when the Nameless Hero and Supersonic were the ones to blame—that only made things worse.

Dad appeared in the doorway to the kitchen. He didn't look any happier to see two superheroes lurking around his garage.

Then something surprising happened. A slight smile formed on my mom's face.

"Here are the rules," she said. "You both wear helmets. You remain far enough off the ground that nobody spots you. And if you're not back home by ten-thirty, we're coming after you."

"And we'll bring our plasma pistols with us," Dad warned.

"You mean you're actually okay with this?" I asked disbelievingly. "Uh . . . thanks!"

Dad stepped forward, slinging an arm over Mom's shoulder. "Have fun."

Five minutes later, we were in the air. Milton soared ahead of me, jets of fire streaming from the soles of his boots. I eased forward on the scooter's handlebars, accelerating to catch up with him.

"Your parents are the coolest supervillains I know!" Milton hollered to me.

"Yeah, I guess they are!"

Giving the handlebars another nudge, I shot forward. Milton surged to keep up. The warm wind rushed over me like a wave. Below us, the lights of Sheepsdale blurred together. Summer was just getting started.

GREETINGS, READER!

Superheroes are everywhere. Leaping across cinema screens, appearing in commercials, and starring in novels like **JOSHUA DREAD** by Lee Bacon.

Okay, fine—I'm not *technically* the star. That would be Joshua Dread, the twelve-year-old son of my archnemeses, the **Dread Duo**. Joshua just wants to be normal, but it's tough to do when your parents are involved in an evil scheme to destroy the world. Especially now that Joshua is developing a strange power of his own.

If you haven't read **JOSHUA DREAD** already—read it now! Because let's not forget, **JOSHUA DREAD** features a celebrity guest star—**me**!

Superheroically yours,
Captain Justice,
Internationally Famous Superhero,
Defender of Justice

Miriam Berkley

LEE BACON grew up in Texas with parents who never once tried to destroy the world (at least, not that he knew of). He lives in Brooklyn, New York. Visit him at leebaconbooks.com.